RIVERSIDE PUBLIC LIBRARY
3 1403 00124 8706

D0114601

RIVERSIDE
PUBLIC LIBRARY
1 BURLING ROAD
RIVERSIDE, ILLINOIS 60546

DEAD MOON ON THE RISE

Also by Susan Rogers Cooper

MILTON KOVAK MYSTERIES

Chasing Away the Devil
Other Peoples' Houses
Houston in the Rearview Mirror
The Man in the Green Chevy

OTHER MYSTERIES

Funny as a Dead Comic
One, Two, What Did Daddy Do?

3/94

DEAD MOON ON THE RISE

SUSAN ROGERS COOPER

A THOMAS DUNNE BOOK

ST. MARTIN'S PRESS NEW YORK

DEAD MOON ON THE RISE. Copyright © 1994 by Susan Rogers Cooper. All rights reserved. Printed in the United States of America. No part of this book may be used or reproduced in any manner whatsoever without written permission except in the case of brief quotations embodied in critical articles or reviews. For information, address St. Martin's Press, 175 Fifth Avenue, New York, N.Y. 10010.

Production Editor: David Stanford Burr

Design: Basha Zapatka

Library of Congress Cataloging-in-Publication Data
Cooper, Susan Rogers.
Dead moon on the rise / Susan Rogers Cooper.
p. cm.
"A Thomas Dunne book."
ISBN 0-312-10448-0 (hardcover)
1. Sheriffs—Oklahoma—Fiction. I. Title.
PS3553.O6235D43 1994
813'.54—dc20 93-45287
CIP

First Edition: April 1994

10 9 8 7 6 5 4 3 2 1

To Don and Evin, always,

and

to my little brother,

Greg Rogers,

with love and affection and

the hope that

dedicating this book to him

will entice him

into actually reading it

DEAD MOON ON THE RISE

◀ 1 ▶

For the first time in my memory, I felt like I was gonna puke. One of those gut-wrenching, from-the-toes kinda pukes you hear about. Judge Lorimer looked at me, waiting for an answer. I knew if my answer was puking on my brand-new wingtips, Jean would be out that door quicker than stink jumps on shit. So I just swallowed real hard and said, "Yes, sir, I do."

The reason I felt the need to puke couldn't have had anything to do with the night before. Sure, I got drunk. Sloppy, kiss-a-toad drunk. But that generally doesn't make me wanna puke. In fact, it never has before. And I had every right in the world to get drunk last night. It was, after all, my bachelor party, and if a pudgy, fiftyish, acting sheriff can't get drunk at his own bachelor party, especially when the wedding was gonna be, in the loosest sense of the phrase, of the shotgun variety, then nobody had a right to liquor up atall, and that's the God's truth.

Then, maybe it was something to do with the conversation that went on last night. The one around two in the morning when the guys I didn't know well or like much, or the guys that didn't like me, had left and it was just me and my buds. My best man had to leave when the drinking started. He's my nephew Leonard and he followed his mama's rule, as he was just going on seventeen.

Now, the conversation might never have started at all if Leonard hadn't spoken out of turn like he did earlier in the evening. What he said was, and he said this to Elberry Blankenship, the former sheriff of Prophesy County and my ex-boss, who's wanted to get something on me for a spell now, "I was surprised Mama didn't throw a fit when she found out Uncle Milt's lady's got a bun in the oven."

I'd been fairly quiet about this turn of events, being as I'm over fifty and I figure I shoulda known better and I figure most of my friends would think along those lines themselves. Not to mention the embarrassment factor. Which Elberry made the most of. Even though he'd promised just a few days before to back me when I ran for sheriff in April, grudges are hard things to let go of.

He got up right then and there and toasted me. "I'd like to propose a toast," he said, and everybody of course quieted right down. "To my longtime friend, Milt, and his lady love, Jean. Now there's some say this thing was a mite rushed, but who's accounting for love? And there's some say as how they can't figure out how a smart lady like Jean McDonnell, a psychiatrist yet, who should know better, could get herself hitched to a lazy no-good like Milt. But then there's no accounting for lust—I mean love." He chuckled. "And then there's some say as a lady plus forty and a man plus fifty shoulda heard something about safe sex—" He turned and looked at me and held up his mug of beer. "Like I said, a toast to my friend, Milt, his lady, Jean, and their impending bundle from heaven."

Which started a lot of jawing and slaps on the back. "Milt, you old dog, didn't know you had it in ya! Ha ha!" "So you ain't been shootin' blanks all them years, huh?" Which I found an interesting point, seeing as how my ex-wife, who I was married to for near twenty years (without even one pregnancy scare, much less a kid) was going to be a mite put out about this whole thing. But then again, why should I give a rat's ass what she thought? Seeing as how she was married to somebody else now. But I'd be a damned liar if I said I wasn't just the tiniest bit pleased that her and her whole damned family were gonna know now exactly whose fault the not having babies was.

Anyway, around two A.M. is when the conversation got interesting. That's when Dr. Jim, our county coroner, said, "Boy, I don't envy you none starting out marriage with a pregnant woman."

Elberry Blankenship let out a hoot. "No, sir!" he said. "Ain't nothing in this world ornerier than a pregnant woman."

Haywood Hunter, an ex-neighbor of mine who now lives in Longbranch after his place got hit by a tornado a while back, laughed. "When Opal was pregnant with our first boy, I 'member one night her waking me up 'bout three 'clock in the mornin'. Scared the liver out of me. I said, 'Baby coming?' and jumped up and put my drawers on. She says no, ain't time for the baby, but she could sure use some blueberry pancakes. So I says, 'Go make you some, then.' So she starts to bawling about how if I loved her I'd go out and get her some blueberry pancakes. At three 'clock in the morning!"

Elberry laughed. "You go get them pancakes?"

"Hell, no. I went in the kitchen and tried making 'em. Messed the kitchen up fit to beat the band, then I go back in the bedroom and she's sound asleep. Goddamn women."

Bill Williams, my good friend and chief deputy of Tejas County, one county over from us, chimed in. "When Mary Sue was pregnant with our first she slammed a cabinet door on her head."

Everybody laughed. "No shit," Bill said. "She had her head in the kitchen cabinet getting out a glass or something and then shut the door. She just forgot to move her head!"

"I was working nights when Shirley Beth was pregnant with J.R.," Emmett Hopkins, chief of police of Longbranch, said. "I come home every night and she's waiting for me pretty as you please. Then one night I come home and she's asleep in the chair. With a butcher knife in one hand and my house gun in the other. Safety off. Scared me to death. I said, 'Shirley Beth, honey, what happened?' Well, come to find out, that's the way she was every night till she heard my car pull in the drive. Then she'd put the knife and the gun up and open the door. I got moved to days for the rest of the pregnancy."

"Ah, hell, that's nothing," Dr. Jim said. "My wife left me every time she got pregnant. And we got five. I'd come in the door and say, 'Hi, honey, I'm home,' and she'd say, 'Who the blazes do you think you are talking to me like that?' Next thing I know, she's packed up and headed for her mama's."

"Yeah, well, pregnancy ain't nothing compared to right after," Bill said.

"Yeah," Elberry agreed. "Only time I ever seen Nadine cry was the first six weeks after a baby. And then again at menopause. Man, that's a bitch."

All the men old enough agreed.

"Yeah, them first six weeks to two months," Bill said, "they're something. Won't let you touch 'em."

"No matter what the doctor says," said Haywood.

"Then if they're breast-feeding, you can forget nooky till the kid's in college," Bill said.

"And no matter how many diapers you change," Elberry said, "come a time somewhere down the road where she throws it in your face that you never changed a diaper in your life and you ain't a fit parent 'cause you didn't carry that baby in your belly."

I noticed all the way through this discussion my two day deputies, Mike Neils and Dalton Pettigrew, both bachelors, were sitting quietly sipping beer, smirking and open-mouthed respectively.

Bill Williams got up to leave and came by to pat me on the back. "All I can tell you, Milt, is living with a pregnant woman's like living with a woman on PMS for nine months straight."

Right before we left, I pulled Elberry aside. "Funny as a truckload of dead armadillos, Elberry," I said.

He grinned. "Now how the hell you 'spect me to keep somethin' juicy like that all to my own self?"

"Well, I might wanna kill you for that, but I still do appreciate you backin' me on running for sheriff."

He slapped me on the back. "Oh, hell, boy, you don't need no backin'. You running unopposed."

"But still, Elberry, your endorsement'll mean a lot."

"Well," he said, scratching his chin, "I guess you're right. And"—he hit me on the back again—"having you as sheriff *would* be better than nothin'."

He went into a belly laugh and I smiled weakly. It was gonna be a long goddamn campaign. Even if I wasn't running against anybody but an empty chair and a memory.

That was last night. Today I stood before Judge Henry Lorimer, a man I knew and respected, with a three-month pregnant lady by my side, and all my family and friends spread out behind us watching. And I felt like I was gonna puke.

Then the judge said, "You may kiss the bride."

I turned and looked at her. The auburn hair with the streaks of gray, the round face with the dimples, the light sprinkling of freckles, her crutches festooned with white ribbons and tiny white rosebuds. This was the mother of my child. The woman I was gonna spend the rest of my life with. I looked at her and smiled. I figured I could handle it.

We'd decided to have the ceremony at a room at the county

community center with the judge officiating. We figured later, after the baby, we'd renew our vows: first at the Baptist church for me, then fly up to Chicago and have another one at the Catholic church her folks went to. I didn't know what my mama up in heaven was thinking about having a grandbaby that was gonna be raised Catholic, but I just hoped she got a little more open-minded once she got up there.

The reception was held in the gym of the community center and, since the bride was Catholic and the groom was Baptist, we decided to compromise and have plenty of liquor but no dancing. Not that Jean doesn't dance. We figured out a couple of weeks ago that with a little work, we could get around a dance floor pretty nicely, even with her legs in braces from the polio she got as a kid and me with two left feet.

We sat at a table to greet our guests rather than a reception line 'cause standing for great periods of time in one place is an effort for Jean. So we sat there and shook hands and got kissed on the cheek a lot from all the well-wishers. Jean wasn't showing yet, so except for the guys at the bachelor party and their entire families and friends, nobody much knew.

Since my ex-wife had sent me an invitation to her wedding, I did the same and I'll be damned if she didn't show up, towing old Dwayne Dickey behind her like a mutt on a chain.

"Milton," she said as she walked up to the table.

I stood and held out my hand. "LaDonna."

She nodded at Jean, who she'd seen me with at her own wedding a couple of months back, then said to me, "Congratulations."

"Thank you." I turned and shook hands with Dwayne. We played our usual game of who can squeeze the hardest and who'll let go first while, with his other hand, he slapped me on the back. "You son of a gun," he said. "I just heard. Congratulations."

LaDonna looked at her new husband. "Just heard what, Dwayne?"

Dwayne had the decency to squirm. "Ah . . ." He looked at me and I went "Ah . . ." right back at him.

That's when my new bride stood up, supporting herself on the tabletop, and said, with a smile on her lips but not in her eyes, "That Milton and I are expecting a baby in August."

LaDonna, for once in her life, appeared speechless. Finally, she just smiled stiffly, nodded her head and walked off, Dwayne tailing sheepishly behind her.

"I thought we weren't going to tell people," Jean said between clenched teeth and a wolfish smile as we greeted more guests.

"I didn't," I whispered. "Leonard let it out last night at the bachelor party."

"Wonderful. Now the whole damn town knows."

"Honey, most of the people in this town can count so they'd all know sooner or later."

As the line of well-wishers had petered out, Jean stood up, slipping her crutches under her arms and said, "I would have preferred later," and stalked, the only word for it, off.

That's when my semi-granddaughter, Rebecca, came running up to me and threw her arms around me. "Grandpa, how'd I do?" she asked.

She had been the flower girl and was still dressed in her pretty pink floor-length thing, looking like the little four-year-old doll she was. "You were great," I said, picking her up in my arms. "You should go professional. I mean it."

She hit my arm. "Grandpa!"

"No, I mean it! Make some money, you do this so good!"

"You gonna pay me for today?"

I reached in my pocket and pulled out a dollar. "Worth every penny," I said. She took the dollar and squirmed out of my arms and ran with it to her mother, who was talking with Jean. Both women were talking, then looking back at me. It didn't take a rocket scientist to figure out my faults were on the top of the list of their dialogue.

Maybe I'd better explain, seeing as how I already said I never had any kids with my ex-wife and now I just said something about my semi-granddaughter. What it is is that Rebecca's mama, Melissa, is the daughter of my late longtime friend and sometime lover, Glenda Sue Robinson, who got killed a while back. When Melissa came to the funeral with little Rebecca, we just sorta became family. Then she got the job working for Jean as a psychiatric social worker and I met Jean and . . . the rest, as they say, is history. Except, if looks could file divorce papers, I'd be divvying up my community property, with the looks coming my way from my new bride.

Why do I do it? Step in it? Every time! I'm a nice guy. I try to please people. I try never to say the wrong thing or do the wrong thing, but, I swear to God, as far as women are concerned, I've never done nothing right in my whole goddamn life. And you can take that to the bank.

I heard a commotion at the door and looked over. There, standing in the doorway looking like a million bucks, was Wade Moon and his wife, Gayla. I hadn't seen Wade in almost thirteen years, ever since he left the sheriff's department to go to work for the Highway Patrol in Oklahoma City. He'd been the sheriff's right-hand man and my biggest running buddy.

"Well, I'll be goddamned!" I said, rushing over and doing the man hug with him. You know the one. Two white nonethnic guys put their arms on each other's shoulders and squeeze. "What the hell are you doing here?" I asked.

By the time he answered, a small crowd of people who knew Wade and Gayla had gathered. "We just moved back. We were keeping it a surprise because I was supposed to show up at the bachelor party last night, but then I couldn't make it." Turning to Elberry, he said, "Sorry, boss. Did I miss much?"

Before Elberry could tell him what he'd missed, I pulled Wade and Gayla over to where my bride sat at a large table with Melissa and Rebecca and my sister Jewel and her family. Jewel and her husband, Harmon, remembered Wade, of course, because everybody in the county had known and loved good ol' Wade Moon. Melissa jumped up to greet Gayla, since they had gone to school together and been in the pep squad one year together—when Melissa was a senior and Gayla a freshman. I'm sure even from as far away as O.U., Melissa had heard the news when Wade had divorced his wife of fourteen years to marry the sixteen-year-old high school girl.

"What the hell you doing back in Prophesy County?" I asked.

"Hell, I retired from the OHP. Me and Gayla came back here to live," Wade said.

"Well, that's great."

"Besides," he said, smiling that Wade Moon smile, bigger than Tulsa, "I hear there's an opening at the sheriff's department."

I smiled. "You want my old chief deputy job?"

Wade slapped me on the back. "Hell, no," he said. "I'm running for sheriff."

◀ 2 ▶

"But I was running unopposed."

"You feel it's a betrayal."

"Damn straight it is."

We were laying in bed, Jean and me, at the Holiday Inn at the Tulsa airport, six hours after becoming man and wife, excuse me, *husband* and wife. And just for your information, there was none of that "obey" stuff in the ceremony either. Jean's idea.

Anyway, instead of talking about our future, about how much we loved each other, or any of that other mushy stuff, Jean and me were talking about Wade Moon. Good old Wade Moon. I, of course, saw Jean looking at him. Just like Jewel was, and Melissa, and every other woman over twelve and under eighty at the reception. That's the way women always looked at Wade Moon.

He was tall, six foot four inches, slim, about 180 pounds, had black hair, now with a little gray at the temples, and a smile that seemed to make women wet their panties. I'd heard more than one woman back in those days say how he looked just like Rory Calhoun. I thought most women liked a more sophisticated type, like me, but . . . Not only that, men liked him too. Wade Moon was a good ol' boy. He was a crackerjack shot, a great hunter, good fisherman, fun guy to throw a few back with. And he used to be my friend.

I never said nothing when Wade was working at the sheriff's department and he used to take three-hour lunches and get me to cover for him. I never said nothing when I saw him drunk on duty one time. And I never said nothing when he started fooling around with a sixteen-year-old girl. But I'd be goddamned if I was gonna let him waltz back into town and take my job away from me.

"I don't know if I should be gone right now," I told Jean.

"You think he's going to get your votes while we're away?"

"Yeah."

"Honey, you've got Elberry backing you. And, as you tell it, that's all you need to win."

"He was backing me before Wade moved back to town. But just barely. You gotta remember, honey, Elberry's still got a bee in his bonnet over me booting him out."

"To look at him now, though, I'd say he was grateful you did, Milt. He seems very happy."

"Nobody's happy about being forced to retire. And even if he is happy, he might still want to get back at me."

"Is that all?"

"What?" I said, leaning up on my elbow and looking down at her. "Is what all?"

"Do you feel there might be another reason why Elberry would want to back Wade over you?"

I laid back down. "You mean like maybe Wade's a better choice than me?"

"I mean, do *you* think he is?"

I sighed. "He's got five years more service than I got. He's got all them years at the OHP. Made it to sergeant there, too. Not all that easy. He's better-looking than me." I stopped, giving my bride ample time to rebut that. She didn't. "People tend to like Wade Moon."

"And people don't tend to like Milton Kovak?"

"Well, yeah, people like me okay, when they think of me, but I'm not the kind they keep on their mind a lot. Wade is."

"So bombard the county with your name and your picture. Campaign!"

Again I sighed. "Hell, I'm no good at that kind of shit."

"Then resolve yourself to staying chief deputy, under the reins of Sheriff Moon."

"I could quit."

"And do what?"

"Emmett'd hire me."

"If he has an opening. You want to go to work for the Longbranch Police Department as a uniform?"

I shook my head. "Maybe we should move to Chicago."

Jean laughed. "Milt Kovak in Chicago! That's a hoot!"

I leaned up again to look at her. "What's so funny about that?"

"Chicago is cold in the winter, it's loud, crowded, and, Milt"—and here she took my face in her hands and squeezed until my mouth looked like a caved in O—"it's full of Yankees!"

When she let go and I could speak again, I said, "Well, hell, forget that, then."

We left the next morning on an airplane to Mexico City, where we got on a train and went to a little town on the Pacific coast Jean had heard about that wasn't yet a tourist trap. Instead of eight million snowbirds laying on the beach, there was only about one million. It was almost pleasant. But I'd never been to Mexico before and I tended to go on a bit about my fears of the *turista.* I made an ass out of myself asking for only Coke in a bottle or a can, brushing my teeth with designer water from the bar, and refusing to eat anything that had a sauce. Jean, on the other hand, against my continued arguing, drank and ate anything she pleased.

On the plane trip back to the States, she informed me our hotel had a bottled water system and laughed like a hyena. I've said it before and I'll say it again, women have strange senses of humor.

We got back to Mountain Falls Road late Sunday night. I noticed the lights were out in Melissa's house as we passed it, something I always look for when I pass by. My way of keeping tabs, I suppose.

Melissa had bought the old Munsky farmhouse down the road a piece from my house. Billy Moulini, the rich guy who has a weekend place up here and bought up all the land except mine a year or so ago when developers were trying to move in, wouldn't sell her all the land, being the gentry-in-training that he was, but he did sell her the house and about an acre around it.

Since babysitter Jewel moved out of my house and moved in with Harmon, after the wedding of course, Melissa's been taking Rebecca into town with her where she's been staying at a day care. Next year she'll start kindergarten and it will be a little easier.

Now anyone who knows Melissa might wonder how a girl who got evicted from her last residence, back in Weirdifornia, for lack of paying the rent, could afford to buy a house. Let's just say Melissa wasn't shy about spending some money her and me came into sorta by accident. My half's still burning a hole in the board of the top shelf of my bedroom closet, hidden in a shoebox. Where it's gonna stay till hell freezes over for all I care. But anyway, there weren't any lights on at her house as we drove on down the road to mine and pulled in.

When my sister Jewel moved in with me 'bout two years ago, she brought furniture, which was good because all I had at the time was a chair, a picture, and a bedroom suite. Then we got vandalized a while back and they managed to ruin everything in the house. The insurance paid up, though, and Jewel replaced all her stuff and I managed to have the floors redone, the broken windows repaired, the walls repainted, and new carpet put in. Then Jewel up and married Harmon and moved out. Now I got clean walls and clean floors, a new chair, a new picture, and a new bedroom suite.

Jean and me lumbered out of my '55 Chevy that had been resting for a week at the long-term parking at the Tulsa airport, and headed for the house. When we opened the door and turned on the light, we got the surprise of our lives. Somebody, no doubt inspired and supervised by my sister Jewel, had gone and got all Jean's stuff from her little two-bedroom in town and moved it all in. And somebody else, probably my new brother-in-law, Harmon, had affixed a little chair contraption to the stairs that would take Jean up and down 'em without her having to crutch her way up. I swear to God, sometimes, cynic that I am, I think about people and just wanna smile. We walked in and looked around. Everything was put up. Silverware in the drawers in the kitchen, glasses in the cabinets, pictures hung on the walls. I looked at Jean.

"Ain't this grand?" I said.

She looked around and said, "Yeah, peachy."

We went through the kitchen into the master bedroom, an add-on after the original house had been built, which just about most of the house is, and saw Jean's bedroom suite, much nicer than mine, all neatly laid out, the bed made, and Jean's clothes hanging in the walk-in closet across from mine. (I peeked in to make sure my little shoebox of money was undisturbed. It was.)

There's this little room between the master bedroom and the original dining room (which is still a dining room and holds Jean's dining furniture real well) and when we opened the door to that, we saw it had been turned into a nursery. Walls papered in a teddy bear print, Jewel's old baby bed from her kids set up with all the stuff a baby needs, a bassinet thing with little T-shirts and stuff, and the cradle my daddy and me had made for Jewel when she was born sitting proudly on the floor in the middle of the room.

I was just about to burst into tears when Jean did it for me and went and threw herself on the bed, flinging her crutches to the floor. So I decided I'd best be a manly man and not join her. In the crying, anyway. I laid down next to her and stroked her back.

"I know, honey, this is just great. Makes me kinda teary too."

She sat up. "What?"

"What they did—"

"This is supposed to be *my* house now!"

"Well, of course it is—"

"These are *my* things!"

"Well, sure they are, honey—"

She jumped up, grabbed her crutches and flew into the kitchen. When she wants to, that woman can *move.* "Your obsessive-compulsive anal-retentive sister can't seem to figure out where she belongs!" she said through clenched teeth. She pulled open the silverware drawer and began grabbing handfuls. "I don't want the silverware there!" she screamed. She ran to another drawer that had kitchen towels in it and flung the towels to the floor. "I want the silverware here!" She flung open a kitchen cabinet and started grabbing glasses. "I don't want the glasses here! I want them . . ."

One of her set of crystal fell from her grasp and smashed on the kitchen floor. She stopped and stood there looking at it, tears rolling down her cheeks. "This isn't my house, it's still Jewel's." She sobbed and looked up at me. "I want to fix up the nursery myself. In about two months. When we're more certain everything's okay. I want my own things. I want to buy my baby's

T-shirts myself. I want wallpaper I've picked out and you've put up! This is our baby, not hers!"

I didn't say anything. I didn't know what to say. In a way, I could see her point. But I knew Jewel. She hadn't done this to be mean. She'd done it out of love. And if we undid it she'd know. And then I'd be stuck between two women who wanted to eat each other's livers. I sighed. Jean must've interpreted that as something negative because she turned around and went through the door to our bedroom, and I distinctly heard the lock snick shut. Yep, married one week and a day and I was sleeping on the goddamn couch. The story of my sorry life.

The next morning I woke up when I heard Jean's car pull out of the new garage. The old one got tore down by a tornado so the insurance paid for a new one. The money wouldn't stretch far enough to replace the garage apartment that had been built over it, so I now just had an ordinary two-car garage. But I did get an automatic door opener. Man, I love it too. Feel like Batman every time I come home and pull in. But Jean, in her hurry to escape her tidy, well-put-together new home, hadn't even bothered to put the door down. I went out on the porch and smoked my first cigarette of the day and stared at the garage.

I was still standing there looking at the incredibly symbolic hole where Jean's car had been when Melissa pulled into the yard in her new little Miata. She's got some nice furniture in her new house too. I figure there ain't much left of her half of that money, which came to $240,000. The girl's smart, just not real bright. I also wondered when Jean divorced me if I was going to be obligated to give her half of my half (the other $240,000) still sitting on that closet shelf.

Melissa hopped her little blond body out of the car, my cat Evinrude following her. He walked past me and into the open door of the house. I turned and watched him walk into the living room and lay down on the sofa, lick his front paw, then settle down to his work—sleeping.

"Well, hello to you too, you big dumb jerk," I said. He ignored me. Evinrude's never been real big on change and leaving him with Melissa for the honeymoon time had been, according to him, rude, crass, and extremely unnecessary. I was sure he'd had to endure a possible change in diet, the entirely incorrect outside environment, and hugs, kisses, and possible dress-ups from Rebecca. Knowing Evinrude as well as I did (we'd shared quarters now for about three years), I figured I'd get his back for a couple of days before he decided to allow me to be nice to him. What a life.

Melissa joined me on the porch. "Was that Jean I saw screaming out of here a minute ago?"

"Screamin's the right word, honey."

Melissa shook her head. "I told Jewel not to do it."

I looked at her. "So this is a big thing with you women, huh?"

"Very big."

"Then how come Jewel Anne didn't know not to do it?"

Melissa shrugged. "I guess her urge to do more than buy you guys a toaster got the better of her."

"You going to work?" I asked.

"Of course. Jean and I were supposed to start riding together, but that can wait till tomorrow, I guess."

"Will you talk with her when you get to work? Tell her Jewel Anne didn't mean nothing by what she did?"

Melissa nodded her head. "I'll give it my best shot." She kissed me on the cheek and smiled. "Don't worry about it, Milt. Half of the mad's just hormones. Of course, the other half's righteous. That's the half you have to worry about."

To change the subject I asked, "Where's my grandbaby?"

"Asleep in the back of the car."

"Don't you wake that child up in the mornings?"

"Wake her up, feed her breakfast, make her get dressed, wash her face, brush her teeth, and by the time I turn the key in the ignition she's sound asleep again."

I walked over to the car, the gravel of the driveway crunchy and cold against my bare feet, and looked in the little space behind the driver's seat where my would-be granddaughter slept like the baby she is.

"Guess I better not wake her up," I said wistfully.

"We'll drop by on our way home tonight. She should be awake by then."

I waved goodbye as Melissa pulled out of the drive and went back into the house to get ready for work. I was running late as it was. Since becoming acting sheriff I was back to wearing a uniform, something I never had to do as head of the homicide unit. I figured if I could lose five to ten pounds, I'd look kinda dashing. Maybe.

According to Mike, Dalton, and Gladys, not much had happened since I'd been gone. Except Wade Moon had been by. A lot.

"I'd forgotten what a handsome man Wade is," Gladys, our clerk, said wistfully. Gladys had never, to this date, said anything wistfully in her life. I figured I just lost a vote.

"Yeah, me and Wade went fishing over to Lake Blue last Saturday," Dalton said, his big, stupid face all grins. "He sure is a nice fella. I remember when he left, I was still in high school, but I remember him."

"There were those who said it was scandalous," Gladys said, which was the most I'd ever heard the woman say at one sitting, and I've known her for close to twelve years, "him running off with Gayla and her only being sixteen at the time. But look at them now. Just happy as larks."

I wondered, but not out loud, how happy Edna Earle, Wade's ex-wife, was to have him and his little honey back in town. When Wade took off, he left Edna Earle pregnant and in debt up to her eyeballs and with a twelve-year-old kid to support. She'd gone to work at the high school cafeteria and been there ever since. She and the two girls, the baby Tula now twelve years old, and her big sister who's twenty-five now and still living with her mama (there's those who say Lonnette Moon ain't right in the head, but I don't know nothing about that) have been barely scraping by ever since.

"Yeah," Mike Neils chimed into my thoughts, "Wade and me's going on a hunting trip next weekend."

"Whatja gonna hunt, Mike?" I asked. "Ain't nothing in season."

"Birds always in season, Milt."

"Oh," I said. I'm not much of a hunter myself. But I'd look it up. I'd dearly love to bust Wade and Mike for killing something out of season. I dearly would.

Other than the fabulous Wade Moon, like I said, nothing much had been happening in Prophesy County since I'd been gone. There'd been a wreck out on Highway 5, course there's hardly a week goes by when there ain't. But there'd been no fatalities. There'd been a fight at the Sidewinder, but then again, there was always a fight at the Sidewinder on a Saturday night. Just business as usual in Prophesy County. There was a report on my desk that Mike had filed saying Lee John Wooley had had three of his Herefords rustled, but then it turned out they'd just wandered onto Davis Montgomery's land and Davis had just sorta neglected telling anybody. He said he hadn't noticed them, but since Davis doesn't run Herefords, I kinda doubt that's the whole truth. Anyway, Mike had handled it nicely and Lee John had only threatened to shoot Davis three or four times before Mike got it sorted out.

I'd been sitting at my new desk in my new office (as acting sheriff, I'd moved into the sheriff's office when Elberry Blankenship had up and retired real quick-like about three months ago) for about two hours, sorting through all the paperwork, when Gladys buzzed me on the intercom to say Wade Moon was there to see me. Oh joyous day. I stood up and plastered a smile on my face to be ready when Wade opened my door.

"Milt!" he said coming in, all smiles and dimples, his hand out to pump mine like we were best buddies. Which we'd sorta been once. Best running buddies. But not exactly soul buds. I guess the only other man I've ever been that close to would have to be Emmett Hopkins. You know, the kinda friend you actually tell things to and who tells things to you. But then again, me and Emmett only did that the one time and we were both drunk.

"Wade, how's it going?"

"Fine. How was that honeymoon?" He smirked.

"Great. Mexico's real pretty."

"Speaking of real pretty, that's a fine-looking woman you got yourself."

"Smart too."

Wade shook his head. "Gotta watch out for them smart ones, Milt."

We both laughed. Then Wade got a serious look on his face. "Milt, you got a problem with me running for sheriff?"

I shrugged big. "No, why should I?"

"You thinkin' of running?" he asked.

"I *am* running. Already paid my filing fee."

Wade pursed his lips and rubbed his chin. "You and me gonna be in competition, huh?"

I smiled and shrugged. "Looks like it."

"Gotta proposition for you," he said, leaning forward in his seat real conspiratorial-like.

I leaned back in mine, getting him out of my space. "What's that, Wade?"

"You drop out now, you got the job of chief deputy for life."

I grinned for real this time. " 'Fraid of a little healthy competition, Wade?"

He leaned back and grinned at me. "Never, ol' buddy. Just don't wanna see an old friend get crushed under the Wade Moon wagon, that's all."

He stood up and headed for the door. Then turning back, he said, "Hey, what're you doing tomorrow morning?"

"Working."

"Naw. Early. Like around six."

"Sleeping."

Wade threw his head back and laughed. "Hey, man, any fool can sleep. Let's you and me go fishing out on Lake Blue. I'll meet you here around five-thirty. Be ready." He pointed his finger at me like a gun and pulled an imaginary trigger, then walked out the door.

What the hell, I figured. If tonight was anything like last night, tomorrow morning I'd be sleeping on the couch and ready to get up and stretch my back by five. Besides, I wanted to know what Wade was up to. I knew there had to be something. With Wade, there always was.

◀ 3 ▶

Jean wasn't home when I got there. Just something I was gonna have to get used to, if she decided to stay married to me. She's the head of the new psychiatric unit at the Longbranch Memorial Hospital. It's a locked unit with twelve beds, most of 'em usually full of people drying out from alcohol or drugs, with a few real crazies to keep my lady's life interesting.

The phone rang as I walked in the door. I almost didn't answer it because I sorta knew who it was gonna be. On the off chance it could be Jean calling to apologize, I picked it up. It wasn't. It was my sister.

"Well?" she said after I said hello.

"Well, yourself," I said, always the great verbal dancer.

"How was Mexico?"

"Great. Just great! Blue water, white sand, blue sky, yellow sun—"

"So marriage makes you wax poetic, does it?"

I laughed. It was the polite thing to do. And my sister and I always try to be polite. When we're not screaming at each other.

"Well, what did you think?"

"About what?" I said. Knowing of what she spoke. Or whatever.

"Milton!"

I started to say, "No, Jewel swung by and fixed it up," but thought better of it. Instead, I said humbly, "Yeah."

Again, the crutches hit the floor and her arms were around my neck. "You are so sweet!" And she kissed me in that way she has of doing that forestalls beans and wienies.

It'll never cease to amaze me how much you can get from books. Now Jean's a well-read lady, being a psychiatrist and all, but until we made love for the first time, even at forty plus, she had no, what you might call, practical experience in that field. But she did this thing. Where she takes my bottom lip between her teeth and pulls on it real light, then starts running her tongue . . . Jesus. Anyway, when I asked her about it, she showed me her copy of a book called *The Sensuous Woman,* and there it was, in black and white. Jean's "I want it now" kiss.

Being practical-minded, I left Jean standing in the foyer, blew out the candles in the dining room, turned off the fire under the beans and wienies, and went back into the foyer. Unfortunately, Jean's mood had switched again (hormones, I suppose) and she was ripping open an envelope, saying "I don't believe this!"

I gently took the envelope from her hand, picked her up in the fireman's carry, which is the easiest way to do it seeing as how Jean's about three inches taller than me, and took her to the bedroom. Her initial protests turned to belly laughs before I tossed her lightly on the bed.

Two hours later the beans and wienies were dried brown crumbs on our plates as we sat in the dining room talking about naming our baby.

"Maybe we shouldn't do this until after I take the amniocentesis."

"You decided to have that test?"

"Milt, I'm over forty. The test is strongly urged on any mother over thirty-five."

I knew about the test. It would tell us whether our child had Down's syndrome or spina bifida, two things babies of older mothers are prone to.

"And what do we do if the test's positive?" I asked. A man's got to ask the question when his wife is a very good Irish Catholic.

Jean sighed. "I don't want to think about it."

"I know you don't, honey, neither do I, but we need to think about it, talk about it . . ."

Jean looked down at her plate. I saw a tear splash in the dried brown gravy, turning it moist. "I want this baby," she said softly.

"So do I," I said. "I want this baby a lot."

"But do we have the right to bring a severely handicapped child into the world, Milt?"

I looked down at my plate.

"You and I will be considerably older than this baby," Jean continued. "There is a good chance you and I, or one of us, could die before it's even an adult. Do we have the right to bring a severely handicapped child into the world and then abandon it? Leave it to the state to care for?"

"We could decide not to have the test," I suggested. "I mean, I've heard this test can be dangerous. Can cause miscarriages."

"It's a one in two hundred chance. But if we don't have the test, then we'd just have to sit around and wonder for six more months. If I have the test, then we know for sure. Then we either do something about it, or have it."

"You've already signed up for the test, haven't you?"

"Yes."

"When?"

"Tomorrow afternoon."

"Can I be there with you?"

Her hand came out and took mine across from her on the table. "I was certainly hoping you'd offer."

We made plans on meeting in her office, since her doctor's office was at the hospital annex, at 2:45 the next day. Then I told her about Wade.

"He came by and *told* me I'm going fishing in the morning. I didn't even get a chance to say no."

"Do you want to go?" Jean asked.

I shrugged. "I'm not much of a fisherman."

"Then call him and tell him no."

I leaned back in my chair and gazed into the hazel green eyes across from me. God, that woman's got pretty eyes. "I sorta wanna see what he's up to."

"You think he's up to something?"

I laughed. "Ain't no way Wade Moon's not up to something."

"What do you think it might be?"

"I don't know. That's why I halfway want to go tomorrow."

"Then do it."

I nodded. "I'll try not to wake you when I get up."

"What time will that be?"

" 'Bout five."

Jean snorted a laugh. "You'd *better* not wake me, not if you want this baby to remember Daddy."

So the next morning I was quiet as a mouse as I crept around our bedroom getting dressed. When I was ready, I debated whether or not to kiss my bride goodbye, then figured I'd better. Waking her, I figured, trying hard to think with what Jean called my "woman" side, would be preferable to not kissing her goodbye. You know how women are.

The kiss didn't wake her up. I thought about nudging her to make sure she woke up and knew I'd kissed her goodbye, then I wished I had one of them videocams so I could record it for her, and then I thought maybe I was a little punchy from waking up too early. I tiptoed up the steps to the kitchen. Just as I reached the door, I heard Jean say, "You're a good man, Milton Kovak." I turned around to see her looking at me, smiling a sleepy smile. I done good.

I met Wade in the parking lot of the sheriff's department. I parked my car and got into his since it had a bass boat hitched to the back of it.

"Mornin', hoss," Wade said, grinning that Wade Moon/Rory Calhoun grin.

"It's awful goddamn early, Wade."

He pointed at a thermos in a tray between the bucket seats of his brand-new, fire-engine-red Firebird. "Coffee," he said.

I poured a cup while he maneuvered the rig out of the parking lot, then lit a cigarette with my free hand.

"Don't smoke in my car, hoss," Wade said, waving the smoke away.

"You smoke!" I said.

"I haven't had a cigarette in five years. Nasty habit."

I tossed the butt out the car window. Until a couple of months ago, I hadn't smoked in almost twenty years and it's totally amazing to me how militant people have gotten about it. You light up a cigarette on a city street and you'll have fifteen people staring daggers at you in a New York minute. You can't smoke in restaurants, 'cept next to the kitchen; you can't smoke on any airplanes. Shit, it's hardly worth the effort. I have this fantasy about in a couple of years you're gonna find people meeting in dark basements with shortwave radios and good exhaust systems, smoking cigarettes and communicating secretly around the country with little bands of the faithful. Coughing into the sacred phlem pile in the corner. I figured I'd best give it up. What with a pregnant wife and all.

"So," I said, "you been going out to Lake Blue a lot?"

"Every mornin'," Wade said. Then grinned. "Course, after I'm sheriff, won't be able to do that so much."

I ignored the dig. "Every morning, huh? Must be nice. Retirement."

Wade grunted. "It sucks. Why else would I be running for office? I mean, Milt, can you see me sitting in a rocker on the porch? That ain't me, hoss. I gotta keep busy."

Yeah, maybe so, I thought, but not busy with *my* job! "So," I said, "you seen Lonnette and Tula since you come back?"

"Oh, yeah, I see 'em whenever I can." He grinned real big. "That Tula, she's something, huh?"

As indeed she was. I guess I'd always really wondered why somebody like Wade woulda married somebody like Edna Earle to begin with. A mousy little thing, skinnier than a whittled toothpick, with about as much gumption as a slug. And their oldest daughter, Lonnette, was just like her mama. Small, mousy, quiet, withdrawn.

But somehow, without even having her daddy around to teach her, Tula Moon was just like Wade. Looked like him, too. Great abundance of black hair, pale skin, big blue eyes, and feisty enough for seven twelve-year-olds. She was the hottest ticket at the junior high and my nephew Carl had fallen in love with her his first day at school. Him and every other twelve-year-old boy in Prophesy County, Oklahoma. She was a cheerleader, editor of the junior high newspaper, editor of the yearbook, and a straight-A student. Tula Moon was gonna be a house afire when she grew up. I almost pitied the man who ended up with her.

"How's she doing?"

"Fine. Edna Earle did a fine job raising her. All by herself and all. I feel real bad about that. Not much of a daddy, I guess."

Being the bastard I am, I said, "Yeah, well, Edna Earle had it pretty rough there for a while. What with no money coming in."

Wade stopped looking at the road and looked at me. "She tell you that?"

"Well, that was the scuttlebutt."

"Well, it's a goddamn lie. I sent that woman money every fuckin' month like clockwork."

I looked at Wade and he looked back at the road. Somehow, I didn't think what he was saying was true. Because I knew Wade. And I knew that Wade had probably *intended* to send money every fuckin' month like clockwork, but just never actually got around to it.

So we talked about the weather, being as it was a nice February day with the sun beginning to rise and sparkle on the dew on the winter wheat planted in the empty fields we passed, and we talked about the Longbranch Cougars' chances at the basketball tourney coming up, and we talked about the change in the menu at Bernie's Chat and Chew, and we talked about that nasty wreck on Highway 5 back when we were working together that took out four starters on the Cougars' football team and three of the cheerleaders and what a bad year the Cougars had had after that. Then finally we were at Lake Blue.

Lake Blue isn't blue. It's baby-shit yellow. But it's the only lake we got. It's in Tejas County and I'm glad because we don't have jurisdiction over it and don't have to worry about harassing the parkers who come out in droves no matter what the weather. Lake Blue tends to keep Prophesy County pretty much parker-free as all the kids would rather drive to the lake to do the dirty deed than park on some nothing country road. What is it about water that brings out the beast in all of us? But, hell, back when I was a semistarter for the Longbranch Cougars, this was where I'd bring LaDonna, night after frustrating night.

I got out of the car while Wade backed the boat down the

ramp. The motion of the wheels of the trailer set up little waves in the water that pushed away the multitude of assorted condoms. I wasn't sure I wanted to eat any fish we might catch in Lake Blue.

We got the boat off the trailer and I held the rope attached to the bow while Wade drove the rig up the ramp and parked it. Then we got in, started her up, and headed out to the middle of the lake.

We fished quietly for about half an hour. Then Wade said, "So, tell me about Lonnette."

I looked at him. "What do you mean?"

"You been around her more 'n me, Milt. What's the story on my kid?"

I didn't know what to say. Lonnette Moon had worked for a while at the five and dime downtown, and I'd seen her there, but she was so shy, or whatever, that she had a hard time even answering a customer, so she'd lost that job. Other than that one, I didn't know about any more. As far as I knew, Lonnette Moon stayed to the house, day in and day out. I'd never seen her date, and I didn't know about any girlfriends.

"Well, Wade," I said, "I truly don't know what to tell you. I don't know Lonnette all that well. I saw her some when she was working at the five and dime . . ."

He smiled. "She had a job at the five and dime?"

I nodded. "Yeah, couple years back. But then she . . . quit . . . and I don't really know what she's been doing with herself since then."

"Well, she keeps busy, you know. Keeping house for Edna Earle while she works. And taking care of Tula. And church work. She goes to the First Baptist, you know."

I went to the First Baptist and I'd never seen Lonnette Moon there. Or Edna Earle for that matter. But I just said, "Well, that's great."

"She's a good kid. Wish she was a little more outgoing, maybe, like Tula."

And then, for the first time maybe ever, I felt sorry for Wade Moon. He was feeling guilty. Guilty about leaving his little girl and her having grown up so shy and withdrawn from life. Like it was his fault. And maybe it was, but she was only twelve when Wade left, and Edna Earle did a heap of raising from that time on. Wade couldn't be totally to blame. Besides, look at Tula. And she hadn't even been born when Wade took off.

"Edna Earle letting you see her okay?"

"Lonnette's a grown woman, Milt, she can do whatever she damn well pleases. And Tula . . . well, she's my kid, like I told Edna Earle. I got rights."

"That's the God's truth," I said.

"Now, Milt," Wade said, his face showing a change of subject, "I don't want this sheriff's race to get in the way of our friendship."

"Well, I'd surely not like to see that happen," I agreed.

"So let's keep it clean."

Like I was gonna start playing dirty politics! Hell, I never played the game at all and wouldn't know the first thing about running a smear campaign. Though I figured I could learn. I'm a quick study.

We got to the lake at six A.M. and left a little after 8:30, making me late for work for nothing, since we didn't catch any fish. But, as I wouldn't have eaten the fish anyway and I got an idea about how Wade planned on playing politics, it wasn't a total bust.

My day consisted of moving papers from one end of my desk to the other until 2:30, when I got ready to leave to meet Jean. The import of what we were about to do was not lost on me. Not on ol' Milt Kovak, superintellect. We were going to find out, in a matter of days, if our baby was "normal," whatever the hell that was, or not. From there would be made the bigger decision. One I didn't even want to think about.

Abortion's a big issue, specially in small towns like Longbranch. With as many Baptists and Catholics as we got, there's a mighty vocal right-to-life group. I've never taken sides. If we had an abortion clinic in our county, which we don't, and the right-to-lifers staged demonstrations there, I'd arrest 'em. That'd be my job. But I don't pretend to know the answer to that question. The one thing that's always bothered me, though, is that the antiabortion crowd seem to be the same people who vote in the politicians who take away the school lunch programs and aid to women and children. Go figure.

I went to Jean's office. Miss Raintree, her secretary, greeted me outside her door. "Well," she said.

I nodded. "Jean in?"

She nodded. If things got any more serious around here I'd probably bust a spleen.

I opened the door and walked in. Jean was at her desk, dictating into a little tape recorder. When she saw me, she stopped and smiled. "Hi, honey," she said.

"Hi," I said, trying to smile back.

I walked up to her desk, leaned over, and kissed her on the cheek. "I'll be glad when this is all behind us," I said.

"One way or another," she answered, standing and getting her crutches situated.

We left, heading for the elevator and the walk to the hospital annex, which was connected to the hospital by way of a third-floor breezeway.

Jean's doctor was Dr. Cannaway. He'd come to Longbranch about a year before Jean had. I knew they'd known each other when Jean was at a teaching hospital in Chicago. Bobby, as Jean called him, had interned under Jean for six months. Although he'd gone on to specialize in ob/gyn, with a subspecialty in problem pregnancies, the two had kept in touch and he'd been the one to tell Jean about the opening as head of the psychiatric unit at Longbranch Memorial.

Alice Anne Mayhaw was at the window when we went in. "Well, hey, Milt!" she greeted.

"Hey yourself, Alice Anne. You know my wife, Jean McDonnell?"

"Well, of course! She's the doctor's patient, now isn't she, Milt?"

Me and Alice Anne had gone to high school together. And she had been a prissy-assed bitch then, too. Head majorette. After half time, when the band and the drill team were set free to hit the refreshment stands, Alice Anne used to carry her baton and march, knees high, to get her a Coke. Me and the other guys warming the bench used to watch her and laugh our asses off. You might say Alice Anne took herself a mite serious. She'd married John David Davis right out of high school. He lasted three months before taking off. Then she married a guy from Bishop named Thompson. That lasted over a year. Her longest. There'd been two others since then, but they were out-of-towners and I didn't keep up.

Me and Jean sat down on the orange plastic chairs and picked up some magazines, *People* for her and *Sports Illustrated* for me. It seemed the manly thing to do.

After about ten minutes, Alice Anne called us to come on back. Sometimes my ability to put up with just about anything without puking is a burden. I figured right then if I coulda, I woulda. And maybe it would have been a help.

I waited outside the examining room while Jean changed into

a gown and Alice Anne took her blood pressure and temperature. Then I went inside and sat down on the little chair while Jean perched on the examining table. We held hands. Not saying anything. What could we say?

Finally, Dr. Cannaway came in. When I saw the way he greeted Jean, I figured Bobby Cannaway hadn't gone to all the trouble of getting her to Longbranch just because Jean had been such a darn good teacher.

Jean introduced us and I stood up and shook hands with Dr. Cannaway. "Nice to meet you," I said, giving him my Dwayne Dickey handshake.

"Sheriff," was all he said. Looking at Jean, he said, "Well, you're looking good. Not much weight gain."

Jean smiled. "Not yet."

"Okay, you know the drill, Jean. Let's hook you up to the ultrasound so we can get a look at this little bugger while we pull the fluids, okay?"

Jean lay down on the table while the doctor began to plug her up to the machine.

"Okay, Sheriff, we're hooking up the ultrasound to get a look at the baby." He pointed at the screen.

Once he got the thing going, I looked real close, but all I could see was a little peanut with a fluorescent pulse Dr. Cannaway explained was the baby's heartbeat.

"Sometimes with just the ultrasound, we can tell the sex, sometimes we can't. But we want to look at the baby now to see where it is so when I stick Jean with the needle, I'll know not to stick it anywhere near the baby."

I nodded. Needle. Nobody said nothing about no needle! He turned off the ultrasound and brought out this godawful long needle, lifted up Jean's gown and started pinching her stomach below the navel, trying to find a good place to stick it. Or grabbing an authorized feel, I wasn't sure which. I backed off and up against the wall, turned slightly to look at a drug company's illustration of the reproductive system of a female. When he was through, the huge plastic syringe was full of yellowish fluid. He set up the ultrasound and we looked at the baby again. Again, it was nothing but a little peanut floating around.

He unhooked Jean and she sat up. "How long before we get the results?" she asked. Jean's never been one to pussyfoot around.

"Well, we have to send it to the lab. The nearest one's in Tulsa and they get backed up. Could be a week."

A week, I thought. A goddamn week. Of sweating, and worrying, and, more than likely, no nooky.

I went outside with the doctor while Jean got dressed, the doctor going to write something in the chart while I just stood there.

Jean finally came out and we left the doctor's office and I walked her to her office door.

"Well," she said at the door.

"Well," I said.

She kissed my cheek and I left. It was about four o'clock when I got back to the office, just in time to get a call about a robbery in progress at the office of Skeeter Trucking out west of Bishop. And it would have been a real tragedy if it hadn't been so goddamn funny. After questioning everybody, taking every statement we could take, the story came out like this:

A little before four, Dorothy Dunn, Skeeter Dunn's wife, was sitting down to work on the books. Anne Louise Watson was filing over in the back corner. Cherie Dosier was typing letters. And Jonelle Jones was clearing her desk because she had a dentist's appointment and was gonna leave early. The door to the office opened fast and two men, both wearing ski masks and carrying sawed-off shotguns, burst into the room. That was the final point at which these guys had any command of the situation.

Dorothy screamed and fainted, Anne Louise screamed and threw her filing papers up in the air and commenced to keep on screaming the entire time. Cherie hit the floor and started crawling anywhere she could, and Jonelle kept thrusting her purse in the robbers' faces yelling, "Take it! Take it all! I don't want it! Take it!"

After about ten minutes of this, Skeeter realized the commotion coming from the office was a little more than the usual, and went to investigate. He found the two robbers, one trying to get Jonelle's purse out of his face and the other trying to get out the door. When the two saw Skeeter, they knocked him down and ran. Without a dime. We called EMS because of Dorothy dead to the world on the floor and all, not to mention the others who were still in quite a state, but a little ammonia brought Dorothy back and her coming to seemed to calm the other women down.

All in all, I felt pretty damn sorry for them robbers. I figured they were both out now at the nearest Burger King applying for real live jobs.

All the excitement at Skeeter Trucking got me late getting home. It was almost seven o'clock before I pulled into the long driveway to our house. The first thing I noticed was Jean's car inside the opened garage. The second thing I noticed was Jewel Anne's car in the drive. The third thing I noticed was this desire I had to flee the scene. Immediately.

◀ 4 ▶

There is nothing phonier in this world than a phony smile. And my bride was doing the best imitation of a phony smile I'd seen in my fifty-odd years. And that phony smile was aimed right at my baby sister. Then, when they both realized I was standing in the doorway to the living room, I got two phony smiles directed my way. Jean's. And my baby sister's. I figured things weren't going all that well.

Phony is as phony does so I smiled real big and said, "Well, hey! Whatja'll doing?"

"Milt," Jean said, still smiling.

"Milt," Jewel Anne said, still smiling.

"Well," I said, still smiling.

"Well." Jewel Anne got up and walked toward the doorway where I stood. Reaching up on her tiptoes, she kissed me on the cheek. "Welcome home, Milt."

"Thank you," I said.

"I have to go," she said and proceeded toward the front door.

"Goodbye, Jewel," Jean called after her, smiling brightly.

Jewel turned around and flashed the toothiest smile I'd seen in a while. "Bye, Jean."

I stood in the doorway, listening to the sound of my sister's feet on the gravel of the driveway as she walked to her car. The sound of the uneven gait left behind when the surgeons tried to remove a bullet from her head. I listened as she opened the car door, listened as she slammed the car door. Listened still as she started the engine, gunned it a moment, then listened as the big old station wagon ground the gravel beneath its wheels as she turned the car around, and listened as she picked up speed on the long driveway and slowed, and listened as the sound of the car grew dim and distant and finally vanished.

Having nothing left to listen to, I turned to my wife. "Well," I said.

The phony smile was but a memory.

"Well," I said again, "Jewel stopped by?"

Still silence. Why was this all my fault? Lord, I didn't do a goddamn thing! Why was this all my fault?

"You want me to fix dinner?" I asked.

"I'm not hungry." She stood up, fixed her crutches, took two steps and burst into tears.

I ran up and held her. Or tried to. She pushed me away. "I didn't wait forty-four years to get married to have my life turn into nothing but in-law troubles!" she yelled.

I nodded my head. "I can understand that," I said.

"What are you going to do about it?" she demanded.

Well, now she had me. I had absolutely no idea what I was gonna do about it. Whatever "it" was.

"Well," I said.

She sniffed, sighed, said "That's what I thought," and marched out of the room, through the kitchen, and into our bedroom. Where I heard the lock snick shut. Again.

Oh, Lord, this was gonna be a long pregnancy.

I was snug as a bug on a skinny couch when the phone woke me up at 6:30 in the morning. I stumbled into the foyer to answer it. Jean was already on the bedroom extension. "It's for you," she said sleepily and hung up. Now whoever it was didn't have to be a rocket scientist to figure out that Jean answering one phone and me answering another at 6:30 in the morning meant there was trouble in paradise. I hoped it was a rude salesman. It wasn't. It was Bill Williams, chief deputy sheriff of Tejas County.

He laughed. "You got them sleeping-on-the-couch-'cause-she's-pregnant blues, Milt?"

"Why the hell you calling at six-thirty in the goddamn morning?"

"I take it you don't got an alibi for what you've been doing for the past couple of hours?"

"I been sleeping. And my cat's been chewing on my toes most of the night so he can vouch for me. What's up?"

"Good question. What's up is Wade Moon. Up to a little more than six feet of water. Unfortunately, the water where he is is seven feet deep."

I sat down on the chair next to the phone. "Aw now, what the shit . . ."

"You wanna get your skinny ass out to Lake Blue? North ramp by the Bait 'n Lunch." He hung up.

At some point Jean must have unlocked the bedroom door because I had no trouble getting in. She was awake and sitting up when I came in to get dressed.

"What was it?" she asked. Like me, she figures calls at that time of the morning aren't exactly social.

"Wade Moon's dead," I said. "Drowned in Lake Blue."

"Jesus!"

"I gotta get over there. That was Bill Williams on the phone."

She rubbed sleep from her eyes. "Lake Blue's not your jurisdiction."

"I know," I said, pulling on my O.U. sweatshirt and a pair of jeans. "Maybe Bill just needs some help with this. Or maybe I'm a suspect."

"What?" Jean almost laughed.

"Well, who had more of a motive for doing away with the asshole? He was running against me, right? And since you wouldn't let me sleep in here last night, I haven't even got a damned alibi!" Hey, I can take a shot now and then, ya know?

I didn't wait for a response, but headed out of the house to my '55 and gunned it out of the driveway. It took me less than twenty minutes to pull the '55 into the parking lot next to the Bait 'n Lunch by the north ramp of Lake Blue. There were two Tejas County sheriff's cars, the Tejas County medical examiner's van, a Channel 17 (Serving the Tricounty Area for 22 Years) van, and a car with one of them magnetic signs saying TEJAS COUNTY SHOPPER'S GUIDE. The press, such as it was, was there. And so were two fishermen and the proprietor of the Bait 'n Lunch, all standing around eating donuts and watching the body come up.

I walked over to Bill Williams and shook hands. "Where's he at?" I asked.

Bill pointed. About fifty feet out was a jon-boat up next to the bass boat I recognized as the one I'd been in yesterday. Two guys were in the jon-boat, leaning over the side with poles trying to get at what was left of Wade Moon. I saw them connect, heard a muffled cheer from the boat, then saw the body rising almost straight out of the water. They grabbed it and pulled it into the jon-boat.

Sometimes I'm a sick son of a bitch. Standing there, watching my old friend's corpse being pulled out of its next to final resting place, a tune kept running around my head. Finally, I stopped and thought about it. Yep, I was humming Creedence Clearwater Revival's "Bad Moon Rising." I cleared my throat and tried to concentrate on the drama out in the water.

One of the deputies in the jon-boat started up the little motor, while the other moved over to Wade's boat, and the two came slowly into the ramp area. Bill and I walked down to the water's edge and waded in to get a look inside the boat. Wade Moon lay on his back, his eyes closed, his mouth open, a minnow wiggling in the little bit of water pooled there. His graying black hair was matted around his head and his wet cowboy boots glistened in the early morning winter sun.

Bill said "Hm," and backed away, letting the medical examiner and his assistant get at the body. Bill and I went back up the ramp and stood next to his car.

"Well, well, well," he said, rubbing his chin. "Where'd you say you was this morning?"

"Funny as a truckload of dead bullfrogs, Bill," I said, then looked back out at the water. "Seems to me he went fishing by himself without a life jacket, which any idiot should know better than doing, fell in and couldn't get back in the boat."

"Looks that way to the uninitiated," Bill said. He motioned to one of the two fishermen eating donuts over by the Bait 'n Lunch. "Lonnie, come on over here a minute."

The man named Lonnie walked over to us, taking the last bite of the donut. "Hey, Bill," he said around the dough in his mouth.

"Lonnie, this here is Milt Kovak, sheriff of Prophesy County. I want you to tell him about finding the body."

"Shee . . . it," Lonnie said and swallowed. He pulled his gimme cap down close to his eyes, then held his head back to look at me. "Me and Jerry Wayne," he said, pointing at the other fisherman standing by the proprietor of the Bait 'n Lunch, "was just out for some early morning fishin' when we seen this thing under the water. Jeee . . . sus Christ on a bicycle! Damnedest thing I ever did see. There he was, just standing there."

"Huh?" I said in my most eloquent manner.

"Standing straight up in the water. The wake my boat made got him to swaying a little bit, but shit, he was just standing there. Under about half a foot of Lake Blue. Me and Jerry Wayne tried to reach him but we couldn't get a good hold and . . . well, shee . . . it. You know, man."

I nodded and Bill said, "Thanks, Lonnie. I hate to make you guys stand around here like this, but I'm gonna need your statements. I'll call over to the plant and let Roy know why you two're late."

Lonnie nodded, spat, and wandered over to Jerry Wayne.

Bill looked back at me and said, "I been pullin' dead bodies out of Lake Blue now for over fifteen years. At least one every winter, two or more in the summertime. And I seen plenty of 'em die with their boot on."

I nodded my head. I didn't get it.

"Boot, Milt. Singular. Man falls in the lake with cowboy boots on, he's gonna sink right to the bottom. The sons of bitches fill up with water and that's all she wrote. Every asshole I ever pulled out of here in cowboy boots had *one* on, Milt. Not two. They sink to the bottom, got enough air to take off one boot. Every damn time."

I shuddered at the thought of it. Trapped on the bottom of that grungy lake, trying like hell to take off your Tony Lamas. Gave me the creeps.

"The reason Wade was standing up in the water? Them damn cowboy boots. Full of water, holding him down like one of them kid toy punching bags."

The deputy bringing in Wade's boat slowed about thirty feet out, leaned over and pulled an oar out of the water, brandished it like a trophy, and sped on in. The medical examiner came up to where Bill and I were leaning against his car.

"How's it look, Homer?" Bill asked.

"Got a bump on his head the size-a Dallas," Homer answered.

Bill looked at me. "Dr. Homer Kemp, Sheriff Milt Kovak from Prophesy County, where the deceased resided."

Dr. Kemp shook my outstretched hand.

"What do you think?" I asked the doctor.

He shrugged. "Lost his balance, hit his head on the side, went in? I dunno."

The deputy in Wade's boat pulled up to the ramp. "Hey, Bill, lookee here!" he yelled, jumping out of the boat with the oar still in his hand.

Bill and I moved away from the car, down the ramp to meet the deputy, a tall skinny kid in his early twenties with jug ears and an Adam's apple the size of a grapefruit.

"Whatja got, Arliss?"

He held up the oar. Even after its soaking in Lake Blue, the oar still managed to hold on to its share of blood and hair. What the dumb-ass deputy had his grubby hands all over was obviously the murder weapon.

Bill looked at me. "Probably been in the water too long for prints anyways," he said, reading my mind.

"Well," I told Bill, "you can take me off the top of your suspect list. I'da had the brains to burn the damn thing. Wood floatin' and all the way it does."

Bill grinned. "Yeah, you'd expect me to expect that, huh? Which means it would be real clever of you not to burn it . . ."

"Shee . . . it," I said, turned and headed back to my '55.

I heard Bill behind me saying, "All in all, Milt, Prophesy County's the most likely place to find whoever done this. Shit, nobody here had nothing against Wade Moon."

I turned around. "You want me to tell Gayla, or you gonna do that?"

Bill rubbed his face. "Well, now, Milt, she does live in your jurisdiction."

"Yeah, but . . . oh, hell, forget it." I got in the '55 and headed to Longbranch. Gayla Moon on my mind.

Twelve years ago, when she met Wade, Gayla Moon had been Gayla Strom. A sixteen-year-old twirler at Longbranch High School. A straight-A student. Homecoming Queen nominee. Runner-up in the Miss Longbranch Contest. A pretty little thing. Bright red hair that fell almost to her waist, iridescent skin, so clear and pretty you thought you could look clear through to her soul.

Her daddy was Ulysses Strom, the closest thing Longbranch had to a celebrity. He'd been an all-star quarterback at O.U. back in the fifties. Did one season with the New York Jets. Then came home and ran for Congress out of our district. Lost, but just barely. Ulysses Strom had married well, to Bernice Cooley, Judge Lloyd Cooley's daughter. Judge Cooley got Ulysses into law school and Ulysses managed, after several attempts, to pass the Oklahoma bar. When Judge Cooley died, back in 1972, Ulysses ran for his seat. And lost. But just barely.

I remember the day Wade and Gayla ran off like it was yesterday. Comes ten o'clock in the morning and Wade still hadn't shown up. Me and the sheriff pacing the rug, wondering what the hell was going on. Wanting to call Edna Earle, see if he was okay, but knowing somehow we shouldn't. Then, around 10:30, Ulysses Strom comes storming into the sheriff's office. This was back in the days when we were still housed in the county courthouse on the square in Longbranch, instead of the new building outside the city limits where we are now.

"Sheriff!" Ulysses Strom shouted, coming in the door. "Arrest Wade Moon!"

The sheriff and I had both come out of our offices at the

commotion and up to Ulysses Strom. "Ulysses," the sheriff had said, "what's going on?"

"Wade Moon's kidnapped Gayla! Find him and arrest him! Call the FBI!"

"Now, Ulysses," Elberry Blankenship had said, "what makes you think . . ."

He was stopped by Ulysses Strom thrusting a piece of paper in his face. I'd read it over the sheriff's shoulder. "Dear Mommy and Daddy," it said, "I'm running away to marry Wade Moon. I love you both very much, but I love Wade more. Sincerely, Gayla."

"Well, this sure ain't no ransom note," the sheriff said.

"It's statutory rape!"

"Well, now, yes, strictly speaking . . ."

"Arrest the goddamn asshole!"

"Now, Ulysses, you got any idea where they may be headed?"

"Put out an APB! Call the FBI!"

And it had gone on like that most of the day and into the week. It was a month before Wade and Gayla were found. His divorce wasn't quite final so they weren't married yet. But when Ulysses and Bernice got up to Oklahoma City to bring their child back, Gayla had told them she was pregnant. Ulysses dropped the charges after that and signed the papers for his daughter to marry Wade Moon when the time came. Funniest thing, though, Gayla and Wade, they never did have that baby.

On their triumphant return to Prophesy County, Wade and Gayla Moon had bought a house in one of Longbranch's newer subdivisions. This one consisted of what they call "patio homes" or "zero plot line homes," which basically meant you didn't get much yard for the dollar. Theirs was a three-quarter brick one-story with a long skinny drive going up to a sideways garage. I pulled up in front of the garage and got out, walking the three or four steps to the front door. I rang the bell and waited. Then rang it again. Finally, the door opened on a dripping Gayla Moon, wrapped in a big pink towel, her red hair done up turban-style, water glistening on that perfect skin, so sheer little blue veins were visible. I couldn't help thinking how drippy her husband was at the moment, too.

"Well, Milt! Hi!" Gayla said, hiding behind the door. "I was in the shower. Can you wait while I put on a robe?"

"Sure thing, Gayla," I said, not wanting to even hint at the bad news until she was decent. Hell, she might drop that towel; then what would I do?

I waited out on the little porch until she came back, her hair combed and wearing a silky-looking kimono-type thing. "Come on in," she said, opening the door wider. "What in the world are you doing out this early in the morning?"

I looked at my watch. It was not quite eight o'clock. "Sorry, Gayla," I said. "I didn't mean to catch you at a bad time. You wanna go in the living room for a minute where we can sit down and talk?"

Gayla Moon had been a peace officer's wife long enough to know that kinda talk. She turned right there in the entry and looked at me. "Where's Wade?" she said.

I took her arm and gently ushered her into her own living room. "Sit down, Gayla," I said.

"Oh, my God!"

I squatted down in front of her and took both her hands in mine. "Honey, I wish to hell I didn't have to tell you this . . ."

"Where is he?"

"Over in Taylor—in Tejas County. It looks like he fell or was pushed out of the boat into Lake Blue. Gayla, I'm sorry, but he's dead."

She pushed me away and stood up. "I'll go get dressed now

and do my hair. Then would you please take me over to Taylor? I don't think I should be driving."

"You go ahead and get dressed, Gayla. I got an errand and I'll be right back."

She didn't answer me, just kept on walking down the hall. I left her house and got in the '55 and sighed. Now I had to go to Edna Earle Moon's house and tell her and her two daughters. Damned if Wade Moon didn't have too many women in his life.

◀ 5 ▶

The town of Bishop in Prophesy County is to the town of Longbranch what Beverly Hills is to L.A. Sorta. On a smaller, cheaper scale. Basically, what I'm saying is, Bishop is where the rich folk of the county live. It's got some poor folk and some middle-class folk. But if you're rich, for some reason, Bishop is where you're supposed to move. And we got four or five rich families, too. My brother-in-law being one. Bishop's about half the size of Longbranch and only about ten minutes away, so I figured I could make it there while Gayla was doing her hair and getting dressed. Not for me to reason why a woman needs to do her hair to go view her husband's body. I've always been of the opinion that there's no accounting for what a woman might do.

So anyway, I hightailed it over to Bishop where Edna Earle Moon and her two daughters lived. There are two trailer courts in Bishop, the good one and the bad one. The good one's got a swimming pool and a laundermat and some real nice trees. All the trailers are newish and well kept and most have little awnings and there's even those with patios and brick barbecue pits. That's not the one Edna Earle lived in.

When Wade'd left her, she had a nice little house in Longbranch they were making payments on. In less than two months, the bank had the house and Edna Earle and Lonnette were off living in a trailer. Where they been ever since.

The court they lived in was called the Holiday Hilton, Holiday Hell by the locals. Most of the trailers were rentals and the residents were mostly people on the move, passing through town on their way to some place worse. I pulled into the court, weaving my unmarked sheriff's car through the tricycles and Big Wheels, past the knocked-over garbage cans with scrawny dogs and mangy cats eating out of 'em, to the back of the lot where Edna Earle's trailer was. I'd only been there once before, three years ago. Checking out a possible witness to a burglary at another trailer. Lonnette had been the only one home and she indicated in her way that she hadn't seen nothing.

It was getting close to 8:30 when I stopped the car's engine and got out and knocked on the trailer door. I was hoping Edna Earle hadn't left for the school yet, but since the government cutbacks, the county had dropped the school breakfast program so maybe she'd be there. The poor kids' loss was my gain. Edna Earle opened the door.

She was just as scrawny as the dogs picking at the garbage in the driveway. Five foot nothing, weighing considerably less than a hundred pounds, she wore baggy polyester pants and a baggy pullover sweater-type thing that had pilled up all over. Her hair, which I remembered as a mousy brown, was mostly gray now, and her face wrinkled up like a crumpled piece of paper when she squinted at me.

"Sheriff?" she asked.

"Hey, Miz Moon," I said, smiling. We used to be Edna Earle and Milt, but that was a long time ago. "Mind if I come in a minute?"

She hesitated, then opened the door wider for my entrance. Lonnette was sitting on the sofa in the living area. Edna Earle went and sat down next to her, indicating I should take the straight-back chair opposite. I didn't know what Lonnette had been doing there. The TV wasn't on, she wasn't knitting or sewing or reading a magazine. Just sitting. Not even looking out a window.

I sat down and looked at the two women who were looking back at me. I cleared my throat. "Tula home?" I asked.

Edna Earle shook her head. "Tula's at school. Whatja want with her?"

"Nothing, really . . . I just wanted to make sure she wasn't here and overhearing our conversation."

"I don't keep things from my children," Edna Earle said.

"Well . . ." I hesitated, looking at Lonette. I was worried about her. About how she'd take it. But that wasn't my concern, it was Edna Earle's. Let her handle the fallout. "Edna Earle, I got some bad news."

She sat there primly with her hands in her lap, not saying a word. Finally I said, "Wade was killed this morning. Looks like he got hit in the head somehow and fell into Lake Blue. I'm real sorry."

Neither woman reacted. Just sat there. Finally, after about two minutes of total silence, Edna Earle stood up. "Thank you kindly for coming by, Sheriff." She walked to the trailer door and opened it for me. I stood up, taking one last peek at Lonnette. She was sitting as primly as her mother had been, ankles crossed, hands in her lap, staring at me. I nodded at both women and left, anxious to get the hell out of there. Those two were spooky.

I got back to Gayla Moon's just as she was coming out the front door, dressed in a black suit, with black accessories, and her hair done nicely. Go figure. She didn't give me time to get out of the car, just got in the passenger side. "I'm ready now," she said.

It didn't take long, getting to Taylor and having Gayla identify the body. We sat in a green-painted room with a TV. There were magazines on a coffee table, but, not so surprisingly, they looked like they had never been touched. I myself couldn't imagine somebody sitting in that room, waiting to identify a loved one and casually flipping through *Time* or *Newsweek.* Maybe *People . . .* Dr. Kemp, the medical examiner I'd met that morning, came out of a door in the back of the room, shook my hand, and turned to Gayla.

"Miz Moon," he said, taking her hand. "I'm real sorry you have to do this." He turned and pointed at the TV. "That's a closed-circuit TV and the only pictures it shows are of the room in there where we keep the bodies. You'll be able to see the body on the TV and make your identification that way."

Gayla nodded.

"Well, okay then," Dr. Kemp said and went back through the door he'd come in.

Gayla and I stood staring at the TV. Finally, it flickered to life, showing only the head and shoulders of the thing on the slab.

Gayla choked back a sob as Dr. Kemp came back in.

"Well, ma'am?" he asked gently.

Gayla nodded. "That's my husband. Wade Moon."

Dr. Kemp nodded. "Thank you, ma'am. I got some papers for you to sign and then y'all can take off. Won't be able to release the body to you for burial, though, until the sheriff's department says it's okay. You understand?"

Gayla nodded and followed Dr. Kemp to the desk by the door where papers were laid out. After signing her name in three places, Gayla said, "I'd like to see my husband now."

"Ah, ma'am, we don't do that . . ."

Gayla squared her shoulders. "My daddy is Ulysses Strom, one of the biggest attorneys in Prophesy County. I would much prefer handling this myself, Doctor, but if you insist . . ."

I waited in the little green room as Gayla followed Dr. Kemp through the door and beyond. When she came out, her eyes red, I drove her back to her house.

"Is there anybody you want me to call for you?" I asked as I parked in her driveway.

"No, thanks," she said, touching her white lace hankie to a tear on her cheek. "I'll take care of it. Thanks for all your trouble, Milt."

"Least I could do, Gayla. I'm really sorry this happened."

She nodded and got out of the car. I watched her until she'd unlocked the door of the house and gone inside, then backed out of the drive and headed for the office.

Everybody was congregated around Gladys's reception desk when I got to the office. When they saw me, they all started in at once.

"Is it true?"

"Wade Moon dead! I can't believe it!"

"What happened, Milt?"

I looked at my staff. "Anybody doing any work around here? Phone been ringing? No crime going on in Prophesy County today?"

"Not so's you'd notice," Dalton Pettigrew said.

I looked at him. Dalton wouldn't know a rhetorical question if it bit him on the ass.

So I told everybody everything I knew. Gladys cried, which it looked like she'd been doing some anyway, Mike's mouth got all prim, and Dalton just shook his head over and over until I was afraid what little brains he had would ooze out his ears. I left the bunch sitting there at Gladys's desk while I went back to my office to sit a spell.

Other than me, I couldn't think of another likely suspect. Maybe Edna Earle. But I figured if she was gonna kill Wade, she'da done it twelve years ago when her passions (such as they might have been) were high. Who else in town had something against Wade Moon? Ulysses Strom. Yeah, old Ulysses sure as hell didn't like Wade Moon. But, like Edna Earle, he'da killed him years ago if he'da mind to. So, maybe, I figured, this didn't have anything to do with Longbranch. Maybe somebody from Oklahoma City followed him down here and did him in for reasons I'd know nothing about. Or maybe Wade picked up that oar his ownself and whacked himself in the head and fell overboard. As likely as anything else I was coming up with. Besides, this wasn't my case. So why was I burning up my brain cells worrying over it?

I picked up a paper on my desk and looked at it. A state form on parolees now living in Prophesy County. How many? How long? Addresses, etc. Well, that wasn't something I wanted to play with. I picked up another paper. An inquiry from Lockland County wanting to know if we knew the whereabouts of a John William Lucke. Nope. Never heard of him. I threw the paper in the trash. A state form on vehicular accidents in the county over the past five years and how they related to alcohol. A lot, was the answer off the top of my head. Shit, I hated that kinda stuff. I had no earthly idea, when I so kindly ushered Elberry Blankenship out of his job, what I was letting myself in for. Those three papers were just the top of a pile that reached about five inches in height. Then I remembered a word I'd heard at a seminar I'd gone to in Oklahoma City a while back. *Delegate.* Had a nice ring to it. I picked up the phone and called Mike Neils' extension.

When he answered I suggested he get his shiny red ass into my office. Except I said it in a nice way. I handed him the paper on parolees and the paper on vehicular accidents, alcohol related, and suggested he get me some figures. I smiled. He grimaced. I smiled again. Delegate. What a concept.

After Mike left, I sat back in my swivel chair (the big swivel chair, bigger than the one I'd had as chief deputy), my arms behind my head, and stared at the ceiling, feet on the desktop. I was doing what I do best. What the sheriff had always paid me to do. Think. I was thinking about who might have killed Wade Moon. I was thinking about the results on Jean's test. And I was thinking about how in the hell to rectify the situation between my new bride and my sister. After half a second of thinking about that, I went back to thinking about Wade Moon. Finding a killer seemed easier than finding a solution to my current domestic problems.

Finally, I flipped my rolodex to O, found the number of the Oklahoma City OHP, picked up the phone and dialed. Other than Wade, I'd known one other guy with the OHP, a guy by the name of Jeeter Post. Me and him spent some time together at a weeklong academy refresher course in Oklahoma City once, then went out on the town together, him being my guide. We got drunker than skunks and had a great old time. Good old Jeeter. When I finally got him on the line and reminded him who the hell I was, he was right glad to hear from me.

"Well, goddamn, Milt, how the hell are you?" he said finally.

"Great, Jeeter. Just great. How you?"

"Great. You in town?"

"Naw. Callin' from Longbranch."

"Where?"

"Longbranch. Oklahoma. Where I live."

"Oh, yeah. That's right. I remember now."

"Anyway. Reason I'm calling. One-a your guys just moved down here. Come back actually. Used to be a deputy here 'fore he went with the OHP. Wade Moon?"

"Moon?"

"Yeah. He was a sergeant with you guys."

"Wade Moon?" I could hear him rustling some papers, then

heard him put his hand over the mouthpiece while he spoke with somebody else. Finally, he came back on the line. "Well, Milt. We had a guy named Wade Moon worked for us but he sure as hell wasn't a sergeant."

"No?" I remembered distinctly getting a note from Wade Moon a couple years back saying as how he'd been promoted to sergeant. I remembered that.

"Hell, Milt, he wasn't even with the OHP. He was a civilian. One of the paper shufflers. Did filing, handled paperwork on wants and warrants. That kinda shit."

I sat there stunned. Finally, after about a minute, I said, "You sure we're talking about the same guy? Wade Moon? Tall, good-looking. Dark hair. Looked like Rory Calhoun?"

I heard him repeat my description to the person in the room with him. I heard a male voice say, "You know, he did sorta look like Rory Calhoun!"

Jeeter came back on the line. "Sounds like the same guy. Why you calling about him?"

"Ah . . . he's dead."

"Oh, well, now, I'm really sorry to hear that." He repeated the information to his friend. "What happened?"

"Looks like murder. I thought maybe it might have something to do with some case he was working on for the OHP. But . . ."

Jeeter laughed. "Now, if he'd died of a paper cut, Milt, we might need to look into that. But otherwise . . ."

"Yeah. Okay. Look, Jeeter, thanks for the information. I gotta go."

I hung up the phone and sat staring at the door to my office. The door opened only two days before by a live Wade Moon. A Wade Moon who'd been a retired sergeant with the Oklahoma Highway Patrol.

You know, he'd been a sorta hero of mine, Wade had. Maybe it sounds dumb. I was a grown-up and all when I met him, but I guess you're never too old for heroes. And he was only a few years older than me. But there'd been something about Wade. Something larger than life. Even the sheriff had looked up to Wade. I got up and left my office, telling Gladys I'd be in beeper range if she needed me and headed out to my car.

I drove the four miles to Elberry Blankenship's house. I hadn't been to Elberry's house since he and his wife, Nadine, had put up me and my family a while back when our house had been vandalized. Before I'd met Jean. Before I'd kicked Elberry out of his job.

I rang the bell and Nadine came to the door. She was wearing an apron over her stretch denim pants and O.U. sweatshirt. Her plump, wrinkled face broke into a smile when she saw me. "Well, Milton! You old married man, you! Come in this house!" She opened the door wide.

"Hey, Miz Blankenship. The sher— Elberry here?"

"He's in his den. Come on back." She started moving down the hall toward the bedroom that had been turned into Elberry's den. "You want some coffee?" she called over her shoulder.

"No, ma'am. Thanks. I'm all coffeed out."

"Don't take much for me anymore," she agreed. She stuck her head in the doorway of the spare bedroom. I could hear game show noises coming from the room. "You got a visitor!" She smiled at me again and headed for the kitchen.

"Hey, Elberry." I stood in the doorway, not sure of the welcome I'd get in his home. Things seemed okay between us right now, but I was never really certain.

He struggled to push his recliner to an upright position. That was the first time I'd noticed it. Elberry Blankenship was getting old. Turning to face me, he smiled. "Hey, Milt. What brings you here?"

"You hear about Wade?"

His grin got big. "Running against you, I hear. Now I'm kinda torn between my two old deputies. You come here to plead your case?"

He didn't know. I sat down on the little love seat opposite the recliner. This was probably the first time something big like this had happened in or around Prophesy County in the last thirty years that Elberry wasn't the first, or at least second, to know about. He wasn't gonna like this.

I told it fast. Just the facts, ma'am. Elberry sat back, staring straight ahead. When I'd finished telling him about taking Gayla to the Tejas County morgue for ID, he said, "Damn. Double damn."

"Yes, sir."

"Bill got any leads?"

"Not to my knowledge."

"You keeping on top of this here?" He looked at me hard. The kinda look he used to give me to make sure I knew what he wanted me to do.

"Yes, sir." I sighed. "There's something else, Sher— Elberry."

He cocked his head at me. The cold blue eyes field-stripping me like a dead butt. "Spit it out, boy."

"I called the OHP. That guy Jeeter Post I met at that refresher course in Oklahoma City back in '85?"

"Yeah?"

I sighed again. "Wade wasn't with the OHP. He worked there and all. But as a civilian. He wasn't no sergeant. He was a civilian worker. Filed. Crap like that."

Elberry looked toward the muted TV set. "Well, I'll be damned," he said softly.

"Yes, sir."

He looked at me for a second, then we both looked away,

embarrassed for our old friend. "You tell anybody else?" he asked, not looking at me.

"No, sir."

"Then don't." He turned his head toward me. "Just don't."

I nodded my head. Another secret shared with Elberry Blankenship. They were piling up like dead bugs after the exterminator. I got up and started out of the room.

"Milton . . ."

I turned. "Yes, sir?"

"Keep me posted." He looked away from me and added, "If you don't mind."

"No problem, Elberry," I said and left.

"If you don't mind," he'd said. Letting me know: He remembers. He knows I remember. And it will always be there between us. Like a turd on the living room carpet. I had to wonder—if Wade had lived, who would Elberry have supported?

◀ 6 ▶

When I got home that evening, Jean was in the kitchen cooking. I walked in the back door and said hello.

She turned from the stove. "Are you all right?"

I sat down at the kitchen table and looked at her. Was this wifely concern, I wondered, or a psychiatric opening? I took a deep breath and let it out. "If you want separate bedrooms, I'm more than prepared to move back up to my old bedroom upstairs," I said. "We can make appointments with each other to have sex. But if we're gonna share a room, then by God, let's share a room. I don't want to be locked out of my own goddamn bedroom again!"

She nodded, adding something to the wok on the stove. Jean liked to cook like that. She'd fixed me wok meals before in her little house in Longbranch. I didn't mind. It was kinda tasty. Healthy, but tasty. Beat the hell out of my sister's cooking, or my own. Jean sighed. "I'm sorry. I've been acting . . . irresponsibly lately. Hormones, I suppose." She sighed again and I saw her shoulders slump and realized she was crying. I got up from the table and moved over to where she stood.

Tentatively, I put my hands on her shoulders. She turned and buried her face in my chest. I put my arms all the way around her, holding her close. Finally, she backed off and looked at me. "I know how it's *supposed* to be," she said, her voice slurred with tears. "I know all about communication and exercises to get two people to talk openly. I know *intellectually* how marriage is supposed to be, Milt, but—"

"But reality can be a son of a bitch, huh?" I finished for her.

She laughed. Then sniffed. Then looked me in the eyes. "Would you have married me if I hadn't been pregnant?"

"Yes," I answered. "Maybe not as soon. 'Cause you'da probably said no."

She smiled. "You love me." It wasn't a question, it was a statement of fact. Something she was finally telling herself.

"More than ice cream and light beer," I said.

She turned back to the wok, stirring. "So, tell me about Wade Moon."

So I did. I sat at the kitchen table and watched my wife cook and told her all about my day. About seeing Wade's body coming almost straight out of the water, the minnow swimming in his mouth, about how that old CCR song got stuck in my brain. She smiled and nodded at that. LaDonna would have frowned and then called her mother to tell her how weird I was. If I'da told her. Which I probably wouldn't have. That was the difference between a good marriage and a bad one. Jean I could tell it all to. She would never judge.

I told her about Gayla, and then about Edna Earle and Lonnette and how strange I'd felt at their trailer.

Jean served our plates and sat down at the table with me. After her first forkful, she said, "I remember one time going with my folks to visit some friends of theirs. I was about nineteen, I guess. Just beginning my sophomore year at Northwestern. This couple had just moved back to Chicago and were staying with her parents while their house was being built. Her parents lived in this little house on the south side. There was absolutely nothing in the house but the barest necessities. No pictures on the walls. No flower arrangements. Nothing. No curtains on the windows. Just plain blank shades. Bare wood floors.

"Anyway, Daddy and his friend went out to look at his new car or something, and Mother had gone into a back room with the wife. Leaving me alone in the kitchen with the old man and the old woman. I was sitting on a straight-back chair. They were standing in front of me. Just watching me."

Jean stopped and looked up at me. "And?" I said. "What happened?"

She sighed. "I have absolutely no idea. I heard my mother call my name from the living room and I seemed to . . . wake up. And there were those two strange old people, staring at me."

"What do you mean, wake up?"

She shrugged. "It was as if . . . I had been out . . . asleep, drugged . . . hypnotized."

I looked at her skeptically. She nodded her head. "I know. I've never told anybody about that day. Except for Dr. Rothkopf." I knew Dr. Rothkopf had been her mentor while she'd been in school. Her psychiatrist when she was going through her training to become one. "We—Dr. Rothkopf and I decided to try hypnosis to see if we could regress me back to that day and find out what happened."

"And?"

She shook her head. "Nothing. The blank incident was still a blank."

"Which means what?"

She stood up and moved our plates to the countertop in the kitchen. "You got me by the ass."

I laughed. I always got a kick out of Jean using one of my expressions. "No, but I'd like to," I said, lunging for her butt.

I got my arms around her waist instead. "You think they were witches?" I asked.

She pulled her head back to look at my face. "No, I never really thought about witches. But do you think Edna Earle and Lonnette are witches?"

"Yep." I nuzzled her neck. "And they put a spell on me. Made me into a righteous stud."

"Oh, really?" Jean said, finding her crutches and slipping them under her arms. "I'm afraid the dishes will have to wait. As a scientist, I need to do a before-and-after study on this," she said, heading for the bedroom.

I followed her. "What?" I said. "You think there'd be a difference?"

Forty-four years of repressed sexual energy can be a bit overwhelming. Luckily I was up to the challenge. Sometimes I fantasize about Jean prior to our first time, fantasizing her ownself about what she'd do if only . . . I was more than happy to fulfill every fantasy she'd ever had or ever could have had. Sex with Jean was always a new experience. Her lust for learning mixed with just plain old lust made for some interesting experiences. But I don't suppose a man should talk that way about his wife. Then again, I don't suppose too many men can. Yeah, I'm bragging.

About nine, the phone rang. I reached across Jean to pick it up. "Hello?"

"Hey, Milt, it's Bill Williams."

"Hey, Bill. Anything new?"

"Naw. You know how slow the district is with autopsies. It'll be a couple of weeks before we get the results."

"I thought they were releasing the body by the weekend?"

"Yeah, but then they gotta actually type up the report, don't you see?"

"Well, I understand they got a computer now. That'll slow down the process a hell of a lot."

"Ain't that the truth? Anyway, I hear you had Gayla Moon down to the morgue?"

"Yeah," I said, holding up the cord while Jean slipped out of the bed and headed for the kitchen, stopping, unfortunately, for her robe, taking the tip of one crutch, catching the neckline of the robe, and flipping it up where she could reach it. "Had her ID the body for the record."

"She say where she was early this morning?"

"I didn't ask."

"Why the hell not?"

"I ain't investigating this thing. He died in your jurisdiction."

"Well, thanks heaps, old buddy. Least you coulda done . . ."

"Yeah, well. Anyway, I went by Edna Earle's place."

"That's his ex, right?"

"Yeah. Didn't ask her where she was neither."

"Jesus H.—"

"Christ on a bicycle. Yeah. I know. What you been doing on it?"

"Getting shit to the lab. Thinking about calling Oklahoma City. See if—"

I stopped him. "Already done it," I said. "Got a contact up there. He said Wade wasn't working on nothing that would have fallout like this."

"Yeah, well, you never know. You get some names of people in the past he's busted that might want his ass?"

Thinking fast, I said, "He worked mostly on investigative stuff. Nothing with repercussions."

"Shit."

"Yeah, I know."

"What about when he was working with ya'll?" Bill asked.

"No, nothing I can think of."

"Well, goddamn, Milt," Bill said, his voice rising, "the man didn't die of boredom, ya know?"

"Bill, this is your case. I'm just helping out."

"Oh, yeah, well, you're a big help. You're still the best suspect I got."

"Fuck you, Williams."

"Hadn't oughta talk to a peace officer that way, Kovak, makes 'em suspicious."

"And the horse you rode in on." I hung up.

I had barely slammed the phone down when it rang again. I picked it up. "What?"

"Well, hello to you too, darling brother," Jewel Anne said.

"Oh. Hey, Jewel."

"You and Jean fighting?" Was there a note of hope in her voice?

"No. Just sheriff's department business. What can I do for you?"

"Well, Harmon and I wanted to invite you and Jean over to the house Saturday night for dinner. His girls will be in Oklahoma City with their mother and my kids are going to a lock-in at the church."

"They're doing what?"

Jewel sighed. She always sighed when I was being particularly stupid. "The youth group gets together and they have a big slumber party. They call it a lock-in because they lock the doors of the church."

"A slumber party? Boys and girls? At a Baptist church?"

"It's supervised!"

"Hell, so's Sunday school and they haven't coed-ed that yet."

Again, she sighed. "Do you want to come to dinner or not?"

"Who's cooking?"

"Harmon's going to barbecue some chickens."

I was mad at my sister. Mad that she'd called when things were going well between Jean and me and now I was going to have to ask my bride if she wanted to go have dinner with the woman she currently hated the most in the world. Then I was going to have to explain to my sister why we couldn't come. "Hold on a minute. Let me see if Jean's got something going."

I put the phone down on the bed, pulled on my pants, and went into the kitchen. Jean was almost through loading the dishwasher.

I kissed her on the neck. It could be my last chance for a while. "That's Jewel on the phone."

"Um-hm?"

"We're invited to dinner Saturday night. The kids will all be gone."

She turned and looked at me. "That will be fine," she said, smiling.

I stood there looking at her for a minute. Should I question this? Should I say, "Honey, what do you really want to do?" Or should I just accept it at face value? Where in the hell was the handbook?

"Sure?" I finally said.

She smiled. I used to love that smile. "Certainly!"

I went back into the bedroom and picked up the phone. "What time?" I asked.

From the kitchen I heard Jean holler, "Ask her what I can bring!"

"And what can we bring?"

"Seven o'clock and a healthy appetite."

"How about some potato salad or something?"

"Nope. Everything's under control."

I'd never heard that particular expression used concerning my sister's cooking.

"Okay, we'll see you then," I said and rang off. Why was my gut in a knot and a little voice saying, "Help me, help me!"

The next morning I got to work in plenty of time to be the first one to make coffee. I liked being the one to make the coffee. That way I could drink it. If Gladys made it, it was so weak it looked like tea. If Mike made it, with his Cajun mama's upbringing, it was so thick you could stand a spoon in it. If Dalton made it, he alternately forgot to add the water or the coffee. I, of course, made it just right.

Around nine I got a call from Millard Running Deer who ran the county animal shelter.

"Hey, Milt. Something weird."

"What's that, Millard?"

"Somebody stole some of our animals last night."

"Stole 'em?"

"Yeah. Gate's busted and three of the pens been busted. Three dogs gone and about six cats."

"You think maybe some drunk just ran into the gate and the animals escaped?"

"Not unless the drunk had a crowbar to pry open the cages."

"I'll send somebody by," I said.

I called Dalton in, explained the situation at the animal shelter, and had him go on by. At three in the afternoon, I met with the county Home Ec lady at the community center to speak to a group of ladies about crime in our community and what we can do about it. Somehow, the topic turned to Wade Moon. Even in death, the ladies couldn't forget about Wade Moon. I'da lost the damned election for sure.

"Have you got any leads in the murder of Wade Moon?" Mavis Davis, my sister's best friend, asked.

"Well, that's not my jurisdiction, Mavis. That's Bill Williams' case over in Tejas County."

"Well, hell, Milt! He lived here! Ain't you looking into it?" asked Loretta Dubjek, a waitress at the Longbranch Inn.

"We are, but we have no leads as of yet."

"What exactly happened?" asked Eva Jean Horne, my former landlady and Elberry Blankenship's aunt.

Again, and again, and again, I went over what little we knew.

"Well, it's a crying shame," said Harriet Crum, retired Home Ec teacher at Longbranch High School, "when somebody like Wade Moon is killed in cold blood in the middle of the lake and nobody can do anything about it!"

All ten women were in agreement on that and the fact that this too, like everything else anybody had ever heard of, was my fault.

I left the community center around four, found a pay phone and called up Melissa. "Can I go pick up Rebecca?" I asked. "I need to talk to somebody who likes me."

"Sure," she said. "She's still young enough."

"Very funny."

"I'll call the day care and tell them you're coming by."

"Thanks. I'll bring her by your place later. Thought I'd go get her an ice cream."

"It'll be good practice," she said and hung up.

◀ 7 ▶

Opal Allen ran the day care where Rebecca stayed while her mom was at work. She ran it out of the old family house, a two-story Oklahoma Gothic with porches and columns and high ceilings. Most of the time I was growing up, the Allen house was painted white. Good old solid white. Now it was painted pink and blue with yellow Mother Goose figures romping around the siding.

Opal was my age, having graduated the same time as me. She'd never married, just stayed at the family house where the Allens had lived for at least three generations that I'd heard of, taking care of an ailing mother, then later, an ailing father. She'd never worked in all that time, but when she was in her midforties, and her daddy died, leaving her the house and little money, she had to do something.

The one thing Opal Allen seemed to be good at, like she told Gladys, who told me, was babysitting. Her four sisters had used her as such all the time she was taking care of her ailing parents. So with her little bit of inherited money and a small loan from the bank, she got her accreditation and opened Opal's Mother Goose Nursery.

It wasn't the only nursery in town, but it was the one everybody wanted. Opal charged a little bit more, but then she was able to hire girls with some actual experience to help out. I was thinking while I was over here, it might be a good idea to sign up Jean's and my baby. I hear there's a waiting list.

I'd been to the Allen house once, my sophomore year in high school, picking Opal up for a dance. It was a Sadie Hawkins dance and Opal had asked me. The way things were supposed to work, she shoulda picked me up, but Opal didn't drive. Leastways, not back then. So I'd picked her up. The date hadn't gone all that well since Opal Allen wasn't what you'd call a big talker. And she also didn't dance. So we'd spent most of the evening sitting on the bleachers watching the others dance, with Opal making a comment now and then about what one of the girls was wearing. It hadn't been one of the highlights of my life.

Back then the Allen house had been full of old and dead things. Old horsehair furniture, paintings of old and dead Allens on the walls, and stuffed dead animals everywhere. I figured then that it had to be an ancient Allen who'd killed 'em cause the cussed things were so old and motheaten they smelled.

But the house I walked into today had little resemblance to the old Allen place. The rooms were brightly painted and had pictures and posters on the walls of clowns, *live* baby animals, and Mother Goose characters. Brightly colored tables and chairs were everywhere, too small for a grown-up to sit in. Brightly colored mats covered the floor in one room and I saw a bunch of little kids, smaller than Rebecca, trying, but not too hard, to nap.

Opal Allen met me in the foyer. She smiled and held out her hand a little timidly.

"Well, Milt, hi," she said, blushing slightly. I hadn't seen Opal since her father's funeral, now close to ten years before. She'd always been one of those scrawny women you couldn't pinch 'cause there wasn't enough flesh on the bones even for that. Her hair had been a limp gray, pulled back in a severe schoolmarmish bun. She'd worn sensible shoes and a colorless cloth coat. That had been the essence of Opal Allen.

The woman who stood before me was ten to twenty pounds heavier, with enough flesh to dimple when she smiled. Her hair was a soft blond, cut and permed, and she wore designer jeans and a brightly colored smock.

"Opal?" I asked, surprise in my voice no doubt.

She grinned bigger and blushed deeper. "Yep. Been a while," she said.

I took her hand and shook. "Sure has. You look great!"

"Thank you. But you're a married man now, you shouldn't be flirting."

I dropped her hand quickly. And grinned. "Sorry, old habits die hard. It ain't right not to flirt with a good-looking woman."

She blushed even deeper and giggled. A sound I thought I'd never hear in this lifetime. Opal Allen giggling. "You're here to pick up Rebecca Robinson, right?"

"That's right."

"Well." Opal's blush faded and her smile with it. "Rebecca's a little upset right now."

My heart fell to my stomach where it did a little jig up against my ribs. "What's wrong?"

Opal pulled me down the hall to what turned out to be her private office. "It's my fault, really," she said, sitting down behind her desk. I sat down in the chair opposite and waited. Opal sighed. "I've always told the parents that the children should not bring birthday party invitations unless everyone in their group is invited to the party. This particular mother told me all the children had invitations. So I let the little girl hand them out. Three children didn't get invited. Maria Running Deer, Angela Rainwater, and Rebecca."

I could feel my blood pressure rising. Could feel the heat in my face. Maria Running Deer, Angela Rainwater, and Rebecca Robinson. They had something more in common than their names all starting with R. Maria was full-blooded Osage, Angela three-quarter. Rebecca wasn't Indian at all. But her daddy had been black. I figured there must not have been a Rodriguez in the four-year-old group, or they'd be on the list too.

"Who's the parents?" I asked.

Opal looked down at her desktop. "Milt, I shouldn't tell you that."

"Who's the parents, Opal?"

She sighed. "Clifford and Maxine Reynolds."

I nodded and stood up. "Thanks for letting me know about this. Can I see Rebecca now?"

We went back into the foyer and Opal went to get Rebecca. When I saw her come out, I coulda spit. Her little face was puffy from crying and her eyes were downcast. I'd be goddamned if I'd let these people get away with this! When she saw me, though, Rebecca's eyes lit up and she ran at me like a steamroller, almost bowling me over. "Grandpa!"

I picked her up in a bear hug and twirled her around. "How's my girl?"

She hung her head. "Okay," she said, letting me know she was anything but.

"How'd you like the biggest ice cream cone you ever saw in your whole life?"

She was down and out the door ahead of me. Opal laughed and I waved goodbye to her. "Milt," she called before I was out the door. I turned. "Don't do anything too terrible to 'em, okay?"

"You saying I shouldn't try out the Chinese death of a thousand cuts?"

She shook her head. "Let the punishment fit the crime. Just five hundred."

I nodded and left.

We managed to get half the ice cream inside Rebecca, a quarter on my uniform, and the other quarter on the seat of the squad car. I was glad I wasn't driving my '55. With the tuck-and-roll upholstery. Before heading back to our mountain, I drove by the office to let Gladys play with Rebecca. It was one of her few joys in life, now that she didn't have Wade Moon to drool over anymore. While Gladys entertained Rebecca, or vice versa, I went into my office and called in Mike Neils.

"Hey, Milt, what's up?" Mike said, eager as ever.

"You know Clifford Reynolds? Owns that RV service and sales over on Highway Five?"

"Yeah?"

"Remember we talked to him a while back about how he stores used oil and all?"

"Yeah?"

"Well, we been getting some complaints. Think it's about time we served him on that."

"You think maybe another warning . . ."

I slapped my hand on the desktop. "That's an environmental hazard! Get the papers drawn up and serve the son of a bitch."

"Sure, Milt." Mike left.

Then I called in Dalton.

"Hey, Milt."

"Hey, Dalton. You know the Reynolds place out in Bishop?"

"Sure. You mean Clifford and Maxine?"

"Yep. Been getting some complaints about all the cars parked around their house. Couple of 'em not even running. Think we need to ticket them cars, Dalton."

"Oh, now, Milt . . . maybe we should just talk to Clifford . . ."

"Ticket them cars, Dalton. Today."

Dalton nodded his head and left. I sat back and smiled. I doubt if it woulda made a pretty picture.

Melissa was already home when Rebecca and I pulled into her driveway in the '55. She came out on the porch of the old Munsky farmhouse and waved at us. After I undid Rebecca's seat belt, she shot out of the car and up to her mother, telling her about the ice cream, Gladys, and, finally, the birthday party that wasn't.

"Well, honey," Melissa said, sitting in the living room with Rebecca on her lap, "maybe Mindy didn't have enough room in her house for everybody."

"But Mindy and I are friends!" Rebecca wailed.

"I know, sweetheart. And I'm sorry. But how about we have a party of our own the same day? Huh? Just you and me and Maria and Angela? How does that sound?"

"Mindy's gonna have a clown."

Rebecca looked at me.

I took a deep breath. "You'll have something better than a clown, baby. You'll have horses."

Rebecca's eyes got huge. "Horses?"

"You bet! Now run along so I can talk to your mama."

Rebecca scooted off Melissa's lap and ran over to me, hugging the first thing she could get her hands on, which was my leg. "Horses! Wait'll Mindy hears what she's missing!"

Then she was off and running down the hall calling for her kitten, who was probably hiding under the bed as usual. Melissa looked at me. "Horses?" she said.

I nodded. "Uncle Rufe. I tell him what happened, he'll open up the whole goddamn ranch to those kids. He's half Indian, you know. His mama was full-blood Osage."

"I just can't believe this, Milt, not after what we just went through . . ."

I nodded. "I thought we fixed most of the bigots in this town. But I guess not all of 'em are as obvious as that bunch before. But"—and here I couldn't help but grin pretty damn big—"I think they may learn their lesson."

Melissa cocked one eyebrow at me, just like her mama, Glenda Sue, used to do whenever she was suspicious of me, which was most of the time. "What have you done?"

I shrugged and tried to look innocent, saying "Nothing," but the grin wouldn't leave my face.

"Milt!"

"The way old Clifford Reynolds stores used oil out at his RV place isn't exactly up to EPA standards."

"Oh?"

"And he's got a buncha cars parked around his place. Out on the street. There's a county ordinance against that."

"I see."

"And once he takes care of that used oil, there's all sorts of licenses needed to run that sales and service shop. And I hear tell how he uses illegals to wash the cars."

"You're gonna harass the poor man to death, right?"

I grinned.

Melissa shook her head. "Don't you feel that's an abuse of your power as sheriff?"

I leaned forward, real earnest-like. "Honey, I'm just doing the job the county pays me for. I won't gig the man once for things that are legal."

"How long are you going to keep this up?"

I shrugged. "Depends on if I get elected."

"Milton, that's terrible," Melissa said, but her lips were trying hard not to break into a grin. I got up and kissed her on the cheek.

"Be good, and I'll see you later."

She walked me to the door. "Remind me never to piss you

off," she said, grinning for real this time. I saluted and got into my car.

I'd barely started my engine when my beeper went off. I decided to go ahead with the half mile to my house before I called in. Jean wasn't home yet when I got there. I went inside and called the office. Dalton Pettigrew answered the phone.

"Milt?" he said, after I'd identified myself.

"Yes, Dalton?"

"We found one of them dogs got stole from the animal shelter."

"Yeah? You call Millard?" I asked.

"Yeah, Milt. Millard's here now. You wanna talk to him?"

I figured talking to Millard Running Deer would be a hell of a lot more productive than talking to Dalton. I said, "Sure, put him on the line."

"Milt?"

"Hey, Millard."

"It was one of our dogs, all right. We tattoo the left ears of all our animals."

"I didn't know that."

"Yeah, we started doing that after one of our volunteers found this one cat beside the road that had been abused terrible. We couldn't prove it was the same cat this guy had adopted from the shelter, or we'da had him charged. Ever since then, we been tattooing them so that won't happen."

"So, was this dog you found okay?"

There was a silence. Finally, Millard said, "Dalton didn't tell you?"

"Tell me what?"

"Damn." Millard was silent again.

I didn't have a good feeling about this. Finally, I said, "Spit it out, Millard."

He sighed. "Dog's dead, Milt. Real dead. I told you we tattooed the left ear?"

"Yeah?"

"Well, we found the left ear about two feet from some of the larger parts."

"Jesus!"

"Real nasty, man. Real nasty. Poor Barnie'd been tortured before they mutilated him."

"Shit, Millard, I'm real sorry."

"What worries me is there's more animals gone, Milt. Where are the others and what's happening to 'em right now?"

"Put Dalton back on the phone, okay?"

"Sure."

I waited until Dalton said, "Milt?"

"Hey, Dalton. Look, you got that carcass?"

"Yes, sir. Got it wrapped in a blanket here in the office."

I shuddered at the thought. "Take it over to Dr. Jim's freezer, Dalton, and tell Dr. Jim we need to keep it on ice and we sure would like for him to look at it, see what he can tell us. Tell him I'll call him in the morning."

"Oh. Okay, Milt. That's a good idea. You think Dr. Jim will do that?"

"You tell him he's gotta. Okay, Dalton?"

"Oh. Sure, Milt. Okay."

"Bye, now."

"Bye, Milt. See ya."

I'd barely got the phone down in its cradle when it rang again, at the same instant my beloved walked in the front door. I kissed her and picked up the phone simultaneously. "Kovak."

"You son of a bitch."

"Don't you be talking about my mama that way, Bill Williams," I said.

"You sorry, no-good—"

"You wanna tell me why you're going on the way you're doing?"

"I just talked to the Oklahoma Highway Patrol," Bill said.

I sat down on the hall chair. "Oh," I said.

"You asshole s.o.b. mother—"

"Me and Mama weren't that close, I swear to God. Now, Bill, I can explain."

"Explain!?! You can explain? Why you lied? Why you interfered in a police investigation? Why you withheld evidence? Why you're the sorriest son of a bitch—"

"Elberry and I decided—"

"Elberry? The ex-sheriff of Prophesy County? Who hadn't got no right at all to stick his nose into *my* investigation!"

"Because of Gayla, you see—"

"This is a murder investigation!"

"Bill, if you'd calm down a minute—"

"You know what, Milton? You know what? I'm liking you for this thing more and more all the damn time! I really am! I mean, you got motive, you got opportunity, you got means, and you got your hands all over my goddamn investigation, fucking it up bigger'n Tulsa!"

"Bill," I said, calmly as possible, "Wade was my friend. And Elberry's. We didn't want everybody to know he lied like he did. He was a proud man, Bill—"

"Proud? You wanna hear proud? You ever hear of Jesse Marshall, sheriff of Tejas County? My boss? Oh, now, Milt, there's you a proud man. So proud he don't like the thought of having assholes from another county all over investigations in his own county, know what I mean? So proud he's liable to fire my ass for this whole thing!"

"I understand that you're angry—"

"Angry? Angry? I'm pissed! I'm boiling! I could fry your liver for breakfast!"

"Bill, I'm sorry I wasn't honest with you."

There was silence on the other end of the line.

"I'm sorry I didn't tell you what I'd found out," I said into that silence. And waited. Then I said, "I'll have my liver delivered to you first thing in the morning."

"You son of a bitch." But this time it was said with a lot less heat. More like resignation.

"I know."

"You sorry-assed mother."

"I know, Bill. I know."

"You get your ass over here first thing in the morning and you tell me every goddamn thing you know! Okay?"

"I'll be there at seven in the morning," I said.

"Good," Bill said. "Wait. I'll be there at eight." And he hung up.

◀ 8 ▶

"What was that all about?" Jean asked, checking the mail.

I hadn't told Jean what I'd found out calling the OHP, what Elberry and I knew about Wade that nobody else did. Now, of course, Bill Williams and half of Tejas County knew the truth about Wade Moon. "Just ol' Bill. Need to go over to Tejas County in the morning and talk about the case," I said. Then I told her about the dog from the animal shelter.

Jean made her way toward the kitchen. "Seems to me you've got enough going on here in Prophesy. You don't need to be worrying about Tejas County. Let Bill do his own job. It will be good for him."

We both heard Evinrude at the same time, scratching on the back door, ready for supper.

We looked at each other, then I went and let him in, picking him up in my arms. "Well, ol' buddy," I said, scratching behind his ears, "I think it might be a good idea if you got grounded for a while."

"Where we going to put him?" Jean asked.

I put him down on the kitchen floor and got his bowl and started mixing his food. "Maybe I should put a box and some stuff up in the upstairs window room. That way he'll be close to outside without really being there."

Jean snorted. "He's never going to forgive you."

"Better that than mutilated tomcat."

I took his dish to the stairs and led Evinrude up. It wasn't difficult to get him to follow me. He goes where the food is. I put him in the windowed room, found a box, set that up, then closed the door. Since his head was ear-deep in his bowl, he didn't notice.

I headed back for the kitchen where Jean was opening the refrigerator. "You hungry?" she asked.

Is the pope Polish? Does a wild bear shit in the woods? "Yeah, I guess," I answered, sticking my head in beside hers to stare at the contents of our refrigerator.

"I need to go shopping," Jean said.

I grinned. "Did you know they opened a new steak house about five miles down the road over toward Tejas County?"

"That's rather decadent, don't you think? Eating steak on a Wednesday night?"

I wiggled my eyebrows at her. "It's either that—or we stay here and live on love."

To give my bride credit, she thought about it. Then we grabbed our coats and headed to the new steak place.

Halfway there, I lit up a cigarette, cracking my window to let the secondhand smoke out. It didn't seem to do much good. Two drags into it, Jean said, "Stop the car!"

"Honey . . ."

"I'm going to vomit! Stop the car!"

I threw the butt out the window, pulled over, and held her while she opened her door and leaned out, puking on the roadside. Finding a Kleenex in the glove compartment, Jean wiped her mouth and said, "I'm sorry. It's just the pregnancy . . ."

I took the pack out of my shirt pocket, wadded it in my hands and threw it out the window.

"That's littering," Jean said.

"Yeah," I agreed, "but it's a hell of a symbolic gesture."

We headed on to the steak house. It was a Mex-Tex steel building with a brick facade and enough parking for busloads of tourists. The owners surely had high hopes. But it was on the highway going toward Texas, if some tourists ever decided to get off the interstate.

The menu consisted of twelve different sizes and cuts of steaks and one chicken dish. They had a salad bar and a baked potato bar. We walked through the salad bar line with Jean telling me what she wanted on her salad. Then she went back to our table while I built us both salads. It's hard for her to work her crutches and build a salad at the same time. I was on my way back to the table when my beeper went off. Half afraid it was gonna be Bill Williams again with another bout of expletives about my heritage, I almost didn't answer it. But I was the sheriff. Acting, anyway. It was my duty.

I dropped the salads off at our table and excused myself, following the sign that said Heifers, Bulls, and Telephone. I dialed the station number and got A.B. Tate, one of our two night deputies.

"A.B. It's Milt."

"Milt, that you?"

"Yeah, A.B. What's going on?"

"I got a call from Millard Running Deer over at the animal shelter?"

"Yeah?"

"They found another one?"

"Tell me about it."

"Don't got nothin' to tell, Milt. Millard said you knew all about it?"

"Yeah. I'll call Millard, A.B. Thanks."

"Okay," A.B. said and hung up.

If Longbranch, Oklahoma, ever ran a Stupid Pageant, A.B. would be right up there as first runner-up to Dalton Pettigrew. Or maybe even be crowned his ownself. Needless to say, it would be a tight race. It would also be a tight race for Mr. Congeniality. But there ya go.

I called Millard Running Deer at the animal shelter. He answered after the third ring.

"Hey, Millard, it's Milton."

"Jesus. Milton . . ."

"What's happened?"

"We found two cats and a peekapoo."

"A what?"

"You know, a cross between a Pekinese and a poodle."

"Oh. Okay. They alive?"

"Not even a little bit. Same way we found the other one. 'Cept this time, the sons a bitches threw them on the front walk of the shelter. A jogger found 'em and called me."

"Look, stay there a minute or two, wouldya, Millard? Jasmine Bodine's on duty tonight and I'll get her to run by and pick up them carcasses and take them by Dr. Jim's, okay?"

I could hear Millard sigh on the other end of the line. "I don't got a good feeling about the animals we ain't found yet," he said.

I agreed and hung up, dialing the sheriff's department number. A.B. answered. "A.B., this is Milt," I said.

"Milt, that you?"

"Yeah, A.B. Listen. Jasmine in the patrol car?"

"Yes, sir."

"Patch me through to her, okay?"

"Okay, Milt. Just a minute."

I waited, wondering how many times A.B. would disconnect me before he patched me through to Jasmine. He musta been feeling sharp that evening. He only hung up on me once. Second try I heard Jasmine Bodine's plaintive voice.

"Milt?" she called loudly, but sadly, into her hand mike.

"Jasmine. Need you to do something for me."

"Okay."

I told her about the animals and asked her to go to the shelter and pick up the carcasses and take them over to Dr. Jim's morgue.

"Tell him to check 'em out and then freeze 'em. And tell him I'll be over first thing in the morning to talk to him."

"Okay" was her only response. It was hard to tell if Jasmine was upset over having to go pick up dead animals, or just in her usual down-at-the-mouth mood.

I walked slowly back to the table, thankful I'd locked Evinrude up for the night, and wondering how I was gonna be in two places at once come tomorrow morning. But I figured, righteously so, that the murder investigation was Bill's business, not mine. I was needed for an investigation of my own right here in Prophesy County.

I sat down at the table with my bride and decided to forget about dead dogs, dead cats, and dead Moons and get down to the serious business of consuming copious amounts of dead steer.

The next morning, at seven A.M., I pulled the '55 into the parking lot of the Longbranch Memorial Hospital, the basement of which housed Dr. Jim's morgue.

He was at a table piecing together a cat when I walked in.

"Hey, Dr. Jim," I greeted.

"Goddamn sons of bitches," he said in response.

"Sir?"

"Look what somebody went and did to a dumb animal! Like they could do anything back! Goddamn sons of bitches!"

In all the years I've known Dr. Jim, and there've been a few, I never heard him wax so eloquent over a corpse before.

"You figure out anything yet?"

He moved away from the cat over to a deep sink where he poured Phisohex over his hands and commenced scrubbing. "Weren't no surgeon who done this. No Jack the Ripper surgical precision here. Hunting knife, I'd guess. Just hacked 'em to pieces. Not before they had a little fun with 'em."

"Do I really wanna hear this?"

Dr. Jim glared at me. "I gotta figure it out—you gotta hear it. Take this cat, for example," he said, pointing to the skinny orange tabby on the slab. "The eyes were poked out while it was alive—"

"Jesus, Dr. Jim . . ."

"The genitalia were removed . . ."

"We're talking some sort of ritual thing here? Like Satanic shit, like that?"

Dr. Jim shrugged. "Could be. Been reading about it in the Oklahoma City papers. Bored teenagers in small towns."

I nodded. I'd heard about it too. It was becoming epidemic. Small communities that didn't have a lot of activities for their teenagers were finding that the teenagers were making up their own activities. Someplace in Texas they actually thought there might have been a human infant sacrifice.

I left the hospital and headed for the high school, calling Gladys on my two-way radio to have her call Bill Williams and let him know I'd be late. I didn't feel like talking to him myself at the moment, for some reason.

Genevieve Greenbush-Snow was the principal of the high school. Far as I knew, old Genevieve was the only hyphen we had in Prophesy County. But I could see her reasoning. She was Osage, of a proud people and proud of it, but then, at the ripe old age of thirty-five, she'd snagged David Snow, a new teacher in town, six foot three inches of hunkism, and she was proud of that too. So we got our first and only hyphen in Prophesy County. I'd gone to high school with an uncle of Genevieve's and had gone home with him on occasion and played with Bobby Greenbush's little niece, a raven-haired three-year-old who liked to bite. We'd kept in touch over the years, me and Bobby Greenbush, and I'd seen Genevieve on occasion and once even thought about asking her out, before Glenda Sue got steady in my life and before Genevieve found her hunkster.

I only had to wait in the outer office for a few minutes before Genevieve called me into her office. The whole place smelled like chalk dust and that crazy sawdust stuff they use on the floors.

Genevieve Greenbush-Snow was still raven-haired, if you excused the strip of white that ran from her widow's peak through the short top part of her hair. Her hair was cut short but nice, her ears showing, with big, dangly Indian-looking earrings hanging from her lobes. She wore rimless glasses magnifying already large brown eyes and had on a loose red top over black slacks. The top pooched out something terrible right around the middle.

I grinned while I shook her hand. "First I heard," I said, pointing at her belly. "Congratulations."

Genevieve smiled back. "You too, I hear."

Genevieve hadn't been at the wedding. Which meant the news was now all over town. If Jean and I had to make the hardest decision of our lives, it was gonna be made even harder by the town taking up sides on what we had to do.

I sat in the chair she indicated while she took a seat behind a desk loaded with papers and books. "What's up?" she asked.

I told her about the business at the animal shelter. Genevieve grimaced.

"You think it's teenagers, right?" she said.

"The thought crossed my mind."

Genevieve shook her head. "I can't think of anybody in this

school who would do something like that. I mean, face it, Milt, over half the boys are in the Future Farmers of America and a good quarter of the girls are active in 4H. Not the kind of kids who would torture animals."

"That leaves half the boys and three-quarters of the girls, Genevieve."

Again, she shook her head. "We have kickers, we have preps, and we have what the kids call 'wannabes.' Those are the ones who wanna be kickers or wanna be preps but haven't made it yet. We don't have any wannabe Satanists."

"I understand your wanting to protect the kids and take up for 'em, Genevieve, but—"

"But nothing! Look somewhere else!"

I stood up. "I understand. But would you do me a favor?"

Genevieve stood up too and headed for the closed door of her office. "What's that?"

"Just keep your ear to the ground. Ask around. See if anything comes up."

Genevieve nodded. "Okay, but don't expect much. Whatever the hell's going on, Milt, I swear to God it's not my kids. Smoking dope, drinking, getting pregnant. Yeah, that's my kids. But not this."

I shook her hand and left, wishing I ever felt as sure about anything as Genevieve felt about her kids.

I called Gladys on the two-way and told her I was heading out of range to Tejas County and I'd call her when I got to Bill Williams' office. Then I took the long way there, going by Lake Blue. I pulled the squad car into the boat dock area where I'd parked when Wade Moon's body had been pulled out of the water. The same place Wade and I had parked the day before when we'd gone fishing together. It seemed like it had been years since that happened. Since I'd worried about him taking my job.

Since I'd listened to him worry about his strange daughter, Lonnette.

I sat in the car and looked at the water, not wanting to get out in the blistering cold February day. There'd been talk that morning on the radio about possible snow. Mostly we just had cold, damp, nasty weather, a little ice in puddles and on some bridges, just enough to cause collisions but not enough to skate on. I pulled my official sheriff's car coat around me, thinking it would be nice to lose a few pounds so I could zip the damned thing up.

I started the engine and headed into Taylor, the county seat of Tejas County, where the sheriff's office was housed.

Now Longbranch is a pretty little town with lots of trees and old houses, some big and spectacular, most small and neat. The Longbranch Inn in the middle of downtown is a picture-pretty place, with balconies and gables in the old Oklahoma Gothic tradition. The bank, first erected in the twenties, was regal-looking, the way a bank is supposed to be. The old courthouse was built about the same time as the Longbranch Inn and is something to behold—from the outside anyway. All in all, my hometown is a pretty place.

Not so Taylor, Oklahoma, county seat of Tejas County. The place is the pits. The whole town was built around the oil boom of the fifties, a temporary place for a temporary boom. Things were hopping so much in Taylor in those days that nobody had the time or the forethought or the inclination to plant trees or build anything that anybody'd wanna look at forty years down the road.

I pulled into the parking lot of the sheriff's office and stopped the engine, sitting there for a minute to steel my nerves for the ordeal to come.

I'd thought about going to Elberry and letting him know Bill had found out about Wade's nonjob with the Oklahoma Highway Patrol. But I'd stopped myself. Elberry wasn't sheriff anymore and although it was sometimes a hard thing to remember, I was on my own now. All grown up. Daddy Elberry didn't have a say anymore in how I did things. Until April, when the election rolled around, I was sheriff. I had to do things my way. I couldn't go running to Elberry when things got a little tight. And with any luck, after April, I'd still be sheriff. Until the next April, or maybe the one after that.

I got out of the car and headed into the sheriff's office, afraid for the first time in my adult life to walk into a house of law. And me with a badge my ownself. Go figure.

◀ 9 ▶

Bill just looked at me, his big ol' moon-pie face just staring daggers at me. I cleared my throat and rearranged my legs where I was sitting in his visitor's chair.

Finally, I said, "Okay, Bill. I'm here for a reason?"

He just kept looking at me.

"I can leave. Just like I got here. Get in the squad car and head on back to Longbranch."

Silence.

"That what you want me to do, Bill?"

Chief Deputy Sheriff Bill Williams of Tejas County, Oklahoma, got up from his chair, walked behind me to the door to his office, and shut it. Slowly he walked back and sat in the chair behind his desk. "Sheriff wants me to arrest you," he said.

My eyes bugged. "Beg pardon?"

"Sheriff says you're the only one in two counties with a real motive for killing ol' Wade. Sheriff says you got opportunity. Sheriff says why'd you lie to us? Sheriff says you got means. Sheriff says won't be the first time in history a peace officer turned bad."

I didn't know Jesse Marshall, sheriff of Tejas County, from the Fuller Brush man. Never met the man in my life and, far as I knew, he'd never met me. So why did he up and decide I was the guilty party here?

"Bill," I said, real nice and slow, "this is the stupidest goddamn thing I ever did hear. The only reason I didn't tell you—not lied, Bill, just didn't tell you—about Wade Moon not being nothing more than a civilian with the OHP was because me and El—because I decided it wasn't nobody's business that ol' Wade had lied about that. Just 'cause the man's dead don't mean his name has to be dragged through the mud—and his widow's with it!"

"Mighty noble of you, Milt," Bill said, leaning back in his chair.

"Fuck this," I said, standing up. "If you wanna arrest my ass, do it! If not, I'm getting the hell outta here."

With that, I walked out of Bill's office. Then I walked out of the building, then I walked to my car. All the time wondering when the long arm of the law I'd served for twenty-odd years was gonna grab me and put me in a cage.

As nothing happened, I drove on back to Longbranch, getting madder and meaner by the minute. I had me a bunch of butchered animals in Prophesy County and I sure as hell didn't need assholes in Tejas County deciding to put my sweet oversized ass in jail. Dammit, I had responsibilities. I was acting sheriff. I was a husband and a father-to-be. I didn't have time to go to jail.

On my way to my office, I detoured through town, stopping at the law offices of Bradley Watts, a fella I'd known slightly for a few years, and had had some official dealings with. He always seemed to get his boys off, no matter what they'd been accused of. I was thinking maybe he was the kinda lawyer I needed.

The building itself was next door to the courthouse, in an old house dating back to the twenties. The downstairs belonged to Watts and the upstairs held a chiropractor and a dentist. I walked into the waiting room of Watts's office, a small space that had in the past clearly been the foyer of a gracious home. Unlike the dentist's office upstairs (where I'd once had a root canal I'd just as soon forget), which had been redone in modern plastic everything, Watts's outer office had been restored to something the original owners might have been proud of.

The shiny hardwood floors were partially covered with Oriental rugs, the walls had wainscoted oak bottoms with what looked like fabric—possibly silk—uppers in pale cream with a fleur-de-lis textured design of the same cream color. There was a camelback sofa in soft blue against one wall, and a couple of overstuffed wing-backed chairs covered in blue and cream brocade with a polished wood table and Tiffany lamp between them. A large antique desk dominated the room.

The little girl behind the desk I'd seen around town but didn't know. About nineteen, bleached blond hair, big brown eyes made up with lots of gunk, cheeks pinker than a clown's, lipstick thicker than shellac. She was wearing an off-the-shoulder red sweater so tight her bosom stuck out like twin grapefruits. She smiled at me and I smiled back. I figured if you took a hose to her, she might be a pretty little thing.

"Mr. Watts in?" I asked.

"Do you have an appointment?" she asked, looking down at her appointment book.

"No. But I'd just take a minute of his time. I'm Sheriff Kovak." I thought I might as well use the clout while I could. If Sheriff Marshall had his way, I wouldn't be able to use it much longer.

"Just a minute," the girl said, getting up from the desk and walking to a large double sliding door at the back of the foyer. I couldn't help noticing that the designer jeans she was wearing looked like they might be cutting off the circulation to the rest of her body. The heels of her boots were so high they made the poor thing swayback. I wondered what she was gonna look like when she reached my age. Probably all crippled up from bad shoes and poor circulation. Then I wondered when in the hell I'd gotten so old I stopped looking at pretty little girls with the appreciation they deserved for the effort, at least.

She stuck her head in the door, came back out, and said, "Go on in, Sheriff."

I smiled and tipped an imaginary hat and walked into Bradley Watts's office, which was as well-appointed as one would expect, judging by the outer room. Antique barrister cabinets lined the back wall, filled to overflowing with legal tomes. Bradley Watts was the only person I'd ever seen in Longbranch wearing a three-piece suit. He was still wearing one.

He smiled and held his hand out over the larger, older desk than the one in the foyer.

"Hey, Milt," he said, smiling. "How are you?"

I smiled and shook his hand. "Fine, Bradley. How you?"

"Can't complain."

He sat and I sat in one of the glove-soft leather chairs reserved for visitors. He had three. I only had two in my office. Course, I got paid by the county and he got paid by people. Just goes to show ya.

Bradley Watts had to be at least my age, fiftyish, but he was a foreigner, having come to Longbranch from San Antonio ten years ago or so. He was a good-looking man, tall, lean, had all his hair. Never did like him much, but he was a damned good lawyer.

"What can I do for you, Milt?" he asked.

"You heard about the murder over in Tejas County?"

He nodded. "A former deputy from here in Prophesy, if I understand the rumor mill correctly."

I nodded. "Yep. Wade Moon. Used to be a deputy with me back about twelve, thirteen years ago. He left here under . . . unusual circumstances. Had a wife and a twelve-year-old daughter, but he up and ran away with a sixteen-year-old high school girl. They came back just a couple of weeks ago. Decided to retire to home. But Wade wasn't really interested in retiring. What he was interested in doing was running for sheriff."

"Against you?" Bradley asked.

"Yep. It woulda been a real interesting race. And because of that, because he was after what some people refer to as my job, the sheriff over in Tejas County has decided he might like to arrest me for the murder."

"I see," Bradley said.

"So, I was thinking, the best thing I could do right now would be talk to a lawyer. See what my options are. See if a lawyer could find out just how serious the sheriff is or if his deputy who told me this was just blowing smoke."

"Mm-hm," Bradley said.

"So," I said, taking a deep breath, "would you be interested in representing me on this?"

Bradley had been doodling on a legal pad the whole time I'd been talking. Finally, he looked up. "No problem, Milt. I'll need a retainer."

"How much?"

He told me and I almost choked, but I pulled out my checkbook and wrote him a check.

Bradley got up and walked me to the door. "I'll get in touch with you as soon as I've talked to the sheriff over in Tejas."

We shook hands. "Thanks, Bradley. And, by the way, I didn't kill Wade."

He smiled. "Doesn't make much difference to me, Milt," he said.

As it was getting on to lunch time, I drove on over to Bernie's Chat and Chew for the daily special. I found a booth in the back, took off my car coat and hung it up on the nail sticking out of the wall, and sat down, rearranging my gun so my butt would fit in the booth. I ordered the special, meat loaf with tomato gravy, mashed potatoes, corn, a biscuit, and a big old glass of iced tea. I was waiting for my food when Uncle Rufe came in the door. I hollered at him and he ambled on over on his bowed legs.

He wasn't really my uncle, just a close friend of the family who I'd known most of my life. He was about as big as a minute but twice as mean, with a hard, leathery face and the phoniest dentures man ever created. They fit so poorly they rattled when he talked.

"Hey, boy," Uncle Rufe said, sliding into the seat across from me in the booth, "I'm so hungry my stomach thinks my throat's been cut."

"That's hungry," I said.

The waitress came to the table and Rufe ordered about twice the amount of food I was getting, and I was feeling guilty about what I'd ordered. But then, Uncle Rufe didn't have a gut hanging over his Sam Browne making him look like Hollywood's idea of a country sheriff.

I toyed with my iced tea until Uncle Rufe said, "Boy, you look mad enough to eat burnt peanuts. What's got you riled?"

So I told him. All of it. And the more I told, the madder I got. And the madder I got, the funnier Uncle Rufe seemed to find the situation.

"Ah, hell, Milty, ol' Jess Marshall ain't got enough sense to pour piss out of a boot with the directions written all over the heel. You want me to call him? I'll tell him. You're so goddamn honest I'd shoot dice with you over the telephone."

"Thanks for the endorsement, Rufe, but I don't know as how it'd do much good. He's got him a sure thing and that sure thing's me."

"You get you a three-piece suit?"

I nodded. "The only one in town."

Uncle Rufe nodded back. "Good. That'll put his bowels in an uproar. Who'd you get?"

"Bradley Watts."

Uncle Rufe sniggered and his teeth rattled. "He's slicker than owl shit. Don't worry the hair off your toenails about this. It'll all come out in the wash."

Thinking it was time to change the subject, I told him about the anti–birthday party Melissa and I wanted to throw for Rebecca and the other mini-rejects.

"Well, sure. I got me some sweet horseflesh out at the ranch be just right for them little 'uns. You give me a holler when you wanna do this thing here, and I'll oblige."

I thanked him and we finished our meals, talking about horses, my sister and her kids, and what Mama would think of Jean.

"Well, she's a tall drinka water," Uncle Rufe said, "but prettier than a speckled pup. Your mama woulda been right taken with her. Even if she is a Catholic."

We left it on that note and I headed back for the office. When I got there, I called the school and left a message for my nephew Leonard to stop by the office on his way home. He had his own wheels, so I didn't think it would be more of a problem than ruining his entire life. But then, most everything did. I figured a kid would know more than the principal who in that school would be playing around with Satanic crap.

I spent most of the afternoon thinking about delegating more paperwork, until 3:30 when Gladys buzzed me to say Leonard was in the lobby.

"Send him on in," I said, and sat back and waited.

Leonard came in, dressed in blue jeans, a button-down blue oxford cloth shirt, running shoes, and a denim jacket, looking put upon and disgruntled. Course, I don't think I've ever seen him where he didn't look that way.

"You wanted to see me?" he said, falling into one of my visitor's chairs.

"Yeah, hey, Leonard, how you doing?"

He shrugged.

"Well, me, I'm doing just fine," I said. "Thanks for asking."

Leonard sneered. He's seventeen. He can't help himself.

"How's your mama and the kids?" I asked.

He shrugged. "Fine, I guess."

"How's Harmon?"

Leonard snorted. Harmon Monk had married Leonard's mama, my sister, only a few months before Jean and I got married. I figured it didn't take long, at Leonard's age, to learn to hate a stepparent.

Finally, Leonard sat up. "Look. I got stuff to do. Did you want something or what?"

"Yeah, Leonard, I did. You're a sharp kid and I know you're in good with the grapevine at the school," I said, knowing neither one was particularly true, but I figured buttering the kid up couldn't hurt. "I was thinking of maybe asking you for some help on one of my cases."

"I'm no snitch," he said, practically laying down in the chair.

"No, no, now, that's not what I'm asking you to do. Just some general information. Just your impression of your classmates."

He shrugged, so I went on.

"You hear about anybody at school getting into weird stuff—like, oh, voodoo, Satanism, witchcraft, that sorta stuff?"

Leonard frowned. "You mean like Ouija boards and shit like that?"

"Well, now, nothing illegal about Ouija boards. Anybody into more than that?"

Leonard shrugged. "Not that I've heard. That whole fucking school's Baptists."

"Watch your mouth," I said. "You're a Baptist, too."

"Can I go now?"

I shooed him away. As he opened the door, I called out, "Sure was a pleasure conversing with you, son."

If he heard me, he ignored it. I left a few minutes later, ready to head home. As I walked out to the parking lot, I saw Leonard with his head under the hood of his VW.

"Problem?" I called.

"Yeah," he hollered back. "It's broke."

"Boy, I didn't know you were so technical-minded."

He walked toward me, grinning at last. "That's real funny, Uncle Milt."

I shoved him gently toward my '55. "Get on in and I'll run you out to Bishop. You can get Harmon to fix that piece of junk for you."

"Piece of junk? It's newer than your car!"

We both got into the car and I poked a finger in his face. "This is a classic. This is a 1955 Chevrolet Bel-Air two-door hardtop. And now that you're getting a cousin, I ain't leaving it to you in the will."

"Thank you, Jesus," Leonard said, looking up at the roof of the car.

I turned the key on in the ignition. There was a shudder, a puff of smoke, and a flame shot out from under the hood.

"Real classic you got here—" Leonard started, but I yanked him by the collar of his jacket, pulling him across the bench seats and out my open door, pushing him in front of me. We got maybe fifty feet when my '55 blew up.

◀ 10 ▶

Leonard squirmed out from under me where we'd fallen when the '55 went up. I could feel the heat from where I lay, getting stronger by the minute. Real strong.

"Jesus Christ!" Leonard yelled and began beating me on the back. "Roll, Milt, roll!"

So I rolled around on the parking lot for a while while my employees streamed out of the sheriff's office looking to see what happened.

"Call the fire department!" I yelled at nobody in particular and everybody in general. I noticed an upside-down Gladys running back into the building while I rolled.

"Okay, Uncle Milt. You can stop now."

I stopped. The minute I did the pain hit me. I lay on my stomach in the middle of the parking lot, wondering if I had any hide left at all on my back. Out of my left eye, I could see what was left of my cherry '55. Black clouds of smoke billowed into the drab February sky. My 265 engine with the four barrels smoldered while flames shot out of the interior, gutting my gray tuck-and-roll upholstery, melting the new '55 Chevy emblem floormats I'd found in the J. C. Whitney catalog. On the outside, flames destroyed the Skyline Blue and Arctic White two-tone paint job I'd just paid five hundred dollars for.

Mike Neils knelt beside me. "Don't move, Milt." He turned his head toward the building. "Gladys, get an ambulance!"

She was running down the sidewalk. "I did! I told 'em to send everything. Oh, Glory, is he dead?" she wailed.

"No, Gladys," I said, "I'm not dead. Get back inside and answer the phone, okay? I'm all right."

"Oh, Glory, Milt, you look plumb awful."

"Thank you, Gladys," I said, my voice muffled by the asphalt.

"Go on and answer the phones, Gladys, okay?" Mike said. "Dalton, you go flag down the ambulance. Leonard, you go inside, use my phone, call Miz Jean and your mama. Tell 'em to meet us at the hospital."

"Oh, Glory," I said, "not both of 'em at the same time."

"You lay still, Milt," Mike said. "I can hear the sireen coming. You lay still."

"Mike," I said, much as I hated to, "you're in charge. You're acting acting sheriff while I'm in the hospital."

"No shit?" he said, grinning big. Then he shoved the grin back. "You won't be in there long, Milt, and you rest easy. I'll do my best."

Oh, Glory, I thought, but I didn't say a word. The pain was something hard to describe. You know how it is when you burn your finger and it hurts so bad you wanna scream every cuss word you ever heard and make up a few new ones? Imagine that all over your back. All over it. All I could do was lie there.

In a minute I heard the ambulance and the fire truck scream into the lot. Then I could feel more pain as the EMTs began trying to remove my clothing. At some point I passed out. I guess that was when the pain got to be too damned much.

I woke up laying on my back, staring at the ceiling. There wasn't any pain. I thought maybe I was in heaven, but when I turned, I saw Jean.

"Hi," she said, leaning over and kissing me.

"I don't hurt," I said.

"Lidocaine. And wet packs. The burns are first degree. Didn't even go all the way through the skin. If you hadn't been wearing that heavy coat, it would have been a lot worse."

That's one of the drawbacks of being married to a doctor. Not a lot of sympathy.

"Well, it sure hurt," I said. Or whined.

"I know it did, honey. Burns are terribly painful. Even the superficial ones."

Oh, great, so now it was just superficial.

"Well, first degree—"

"Isn't bad at all."

"Leonard okay?"

"He's out in the hall waiting to see you. His nose was broken when the two of you hit the ground, but it's a minor break, he shouldn't need rhinoplasty."

I nodded my head. "How long they gonna keep me in here?"

"At least overnight. I can probably take you home tomorrow. We'll get a home-duty nurse to come out to change your dressings while I'm at work."

"Just make sure she's cute," I said, then fell asleep.

When I woke up again, Jewel was sitting where Jean had been.

"Where's Jean?" I asked.

"One of her patients took a swing at one of the orderlies. She'll be back as soon as she can. How're you feeling?"

It hurt. Lord God, did it hurt. "It hurts," I said.

Jewel rang for the nurse. "It's probably time for more medicine."

"Leonard's nose okay?" I asked.

She smiled. "Yeah. He was hoping it would leave a permanent bump to give him character, but no such luck."

"Sorry about almost blowing up your kid."

"Yeah, when you're better, we're gonna have to talk about that."

The nurse came in and made Jewel leave. Then she gave me a pill, rolled me over on my side while I screamed inwardly—and maybe a little outwardly—and changed the packs and dressings. Then rolled me back. I was hoping this wouldn't be the nurse I got at home. She had the touch of Sherman marching through Georgia.

In a minute, I dozed off again.

When I woke up, Jean was back in the chair. "How's your patient?" I asked.

"Crazy," she said.

"Where's Jewel?"

"She took Leonard home. She'll come by the house tomorrow after we get you home."

I nodded.

"Are you in any pain?" Jean asked.

I thought for a minute. "No," I said. "Not really."

She smiled. "Good."

I looked at her stomach. "How's junior?" I asked.

"Worried about his daddy."

There was a tentative knock on the door. Jean struggled out of her chair, grabbing her crutches, and opened the wide hospital door.

I could hear Mike Neils outside the door. "How's he doing?"

"Come on in, Mike. I got some questions!" I said.

Mike came in and pulled up the chair from the empty bed next to mine and sat down.

"How you doing, Milt?"

"Okay. Did you have the '55 checked out?"

He nodded. "Incendiary device attached to the cylinder block.

Not a very good one, thank God. If the guy'd known what he was doing, well . . ."

"You'd be scraping me off the asphalt. Leonard, too."

There was another knock on the door. Mike got up to answer it, and backed sheepishly away as Melissa came in.

"Hi, Mike," she said.

"Hi, Melissa," he said, turning scarlet.

Oh, great, I thought.

Melissa came over to my bed and kissed Jean and then me on the cheeks. "Hey, cowboy, you been playing rough again?" she said, grinning from ear to ear.

Mike was standing with his hands on the back of the chair he'd vacated. "Here, Melissa, have a seat," he said, and blushed.

"Thanks, Mike," she said, smiling.

I'd have to have a talk with the girl, the way she was leading that poor boy on. Acting like she liked him.

"Well, Milt," Mike said, and cleared his throat. "Well, I guess I'd better get back to the shop. Now that I'm acting sheriff and all."

He looked at Melissa for her reaction. "Wise choice, Milt," she said to me, while looking at Mike Neils, the most annoying person I'd ever met. And she smiled. I could tell this was not a good omen of things to come. My mind raced ahead ten years—to barbecues and birthday parties and Christmas dinner. All spent with Mike Neils telling endless stories about boring people and nonevents. I was gonna have to nip this in the bud.

I fell asleep on that thought.

The next morning, armed with tubes of lidocaine, prescription bottles, and wet packs (having a wife on staff at the particular hospital got us some good deals), along with the one plant I'd got (sent by Gladys and charged to the county), we headed out of the hospital, me in a wheelchair and Jean on her crutches. Jean's car was pulled up to the front of the hospital, we got in, and Jean drove us home.

I was quiet on the way back to my mountain, mourning my '55. I'd had that car since 1959. I'd bought it wrecked off a guy who thought it was totaled. Me and my old best friend, Linn Robinson, had done all the work ourselves, buying a new hood, taillights, and driver's-side door from a wrecking yard, and stealing a wheel rim from old man Marshand who lived two doors down from Linn and drove a cherry '55 his ownself. We'd primered it and then driven it over to Linn's uncle's paint shop. He wouldn't give us a free paint job, but told us we could paint it ourselves after-hours with whatever we could find in the leftover paints.

There were dozens upon dozens of paint cans on the walls, every imaginable color. But not enough of any one color to do the whole car. After two six-packs of beer swiped out of Linn's uncle's cooler, we decided the best thing to do would be to mix all the paints together. We poured them all into a big bucket, used the automatic mixer to stir it together, and, lo and behold, came up with a really pretty gold color. We spent all night painting the '55, then the next afternoon after school we put the golden lovely into the baking oven to harden. What came out several hours later was the ugliest baby-shit brown color you ever saw.

I drove it that way all those years. Never having had the extra money to bring my baby back to new. But just a few months ago, with my first check as acting sheriff, I'd gone to Tulsa and had it done. And finally, after all those years, my '55 had been really, really cherry. Like a buck-toothed fourteen-year-old with a bad personality. At that moment, I couldn't tell which hurt worse, my back or my soul.

We pulled up to the house where we were greeted by a lady of about two hundred pounds or so, somewhere around sixty, wearing a white nurse's uniform. I gotta admit though, when she smiled, she *was* cute, so I can't say my bride went totally against my wishes.

"Hello, Sheriff," she greeted me, her smile bright. "How are we feeling this mornin'?"

I crawled gingerly out of Jean's car. "Like shit," I said, walking by her into the house.

"Does Doctor plan on going back to the hospital now?" the nurse asked Jean.

"Yes, Martha. I'll leave him in your capable hands. He'll probably sleep most of the day."

"We'll make sure he's just as comfortable as can be," Nurse Martha said, smiling.

I refrained from asking if she had a turd in her pocket. I woulda been proud of myself for the restraint, except it just hurt too damn bad to make remarks. I kissed Jean goodbye and headed for the bedroom.

Nurse Martha was there before I got there. "Here, let's get those clothes off you and get something on that'll make us a little more comfortable," she said, pushing me to the bed and lifting my feet to take my shoes off.

I got settled in a loose T-shirt and my boxers, my legs covered by the sheet and blanket, the pill taken and the wet packs under my back. Still, Nurse Martha hovered.

"Thank you very much, ma'am," I said. "I think I can take it from here."

"Are you hungry, Sheriff?"

"No, ma'am, not at the moment."

"How about a nice cup of tea?"

"No, thanks."

"A soda?" she persisted.

"No!" I counted to ten. "No, really, I'm fine. Why don't you go in the living room and watch TV?"

She bristled. "I don't watch TV while I'm on duty," she said stiffly. Then she smiled. I knew that, soon, I would come to hate that smile. She pulled up a chair and sat down. "I'll just stay here with you until you fall asleep."

"Martha? Is that right, it's Martha?"

She smiled. "Yes, Sheriff. Martha Pruitt."

"Abel Pruitt's wife?"

She smiled. "Abel's my brother-in-law. Jesse was my husband, Abel's older brother, but he passed on four years ago."

"I'm sorry," I said.

"Thank you," she said.

Pruitt's Auto Shop had worked on my '55 a number of times. Tune-ups, a new fuel pump. They did good work. "Jesse worked with Abel at the auto shop, right?"

"Yes, they were partners. Jesse was a wonderful mechanic."

"Yes, he was," I admitted. "Mrs. Pruitt . . ."

"Martha, please."

"Martha. I really need some alone time right now, know what I mean? I have some thinking to do before these pills kick in and put me out. Would you mind . . . ?"

She smiled. "Well, not at all, Sheriff. I'm sure you've got things on your mind, after all that's happened. But you rest assured," she said at the doorway, "that that pretty Chevrolet of yours is up in heaven with Jesse."

I never doubted for a minute that the '55 had a soul, but I did doubt that heaven had room for automobiles.

After she'd left, I picked up the bedside phone and dialed the sheriff's department and, after assuring Gladys that, no, I wasn't dead, and yes, I would be okay eventually, got to speak to Mike Neils.

"Any prints?" I asked.

"On what? Wasn't much left to print. By the way, Bill Williams called up here madder than a wet hen, but after Gladys told him what happened to you, he calmed down and said something kinda strange."

My stomach got a little queasy. "Like what?"

"He said he'd tell his sheriff he could rest easy 'cause you were out of commission. What'd he mean by that, Milt?"

"God only knows, Mike. Listen, anything left of the '55?"

"Not even the steering wheel."

"Wonderful. Okay. Listen . . ."

"Yeah, Milt?"

I couldn't think of anything to tell him to do, so I just said, "Well, if anything comes up you can't handle, call me. Okay?"

"No problem, Milt. Will do. Get better, hear?"

"Right," I said and hung up.

Evinrude marched into the room and up to the side of the bed, where he turned and gave me his back. He obviously understood that I was hurt and couldn't come to him. So he very graciously came to me to show me his disdain.

"I don't care how pissed you get," I told him, "you can't go outside while there's a maniac out there killing animals. You understand?"

He didn't move a muscle. His back was a mass of orange tabby stripes totally ignoring me.

"Did Martha feed you?" I asked.

Still he said nothing. "Well, forget you," I told him. "I don't need this." I rolled over on my other side, giving him my back. Two could play at that game.

My mind had other things to think about than a pissed-off cat. Somebody had put a bomb in my '55. An inept somebody, or I'd be dead. The only things I had going right now that could piss somebody off that much were the deal with the dead animals and Wade Moon's murder. And that wasn't even my jurisdiction. If somebody was pissed off about that, why in the hell didn't they try blowing up Bill Williams?

It was definitely one or the other. Wade Moon or the dead pussycats. Dead pussycats and dead dogs. And dead Moons. Dead moons and dead '55s. Kitty cats and puppy dogs. The pill kicked in and I kicked out.

◀ 11 ▶

It took a week of laying around before the doctor said I could go back to work. He released me the same day Jean's doctor was supposed to tell us the results of the amniocentesis.

I called the office and told them I'd be in late or, maybe, not at all. Jean had cleared her schedule. If it was bad news, she felt she wouldn't be able to work. I sorta agreed with her.

At nine A.M., we drove together in her car to the hospital and walked up to Dr. Cannaway's office in the annex. We sat in the waiting room, neither of us even pretending to read the magazines. Finally, twenty minutes after our appointed time, the nurse called us in. We went straight to Dr. Cannaway's private office and sat, waiting again. Ten minutes later, he came in.

"Jean! How are you?"

"Fine, Bobby, how are you?" Jean said, showing a calm I envied.

"Sheriff?" the doctor asked.

"Fine," I said shortly.

He opened a file and looked down at it. "Well, I've got good news and I've got bad news."

He looked up. Jean and I both stared at him, neither of us daring to look at each other.

"The good news is, the baby's fine. No signs of Down's or

spina bifida or anything else. The bad news is, by the time this boy's in college, it's gonna run you a hundred grand!" And then he smiled.

"The baby's okay?" Jean said, oblivious to his joke.

"The baby is A-okay," Dr. Cannaway said.

"A boy?" I said. "You said a boy?"

He grinned. "Definitely a boy."

Jean and I looked at each other. Then our arms were around each other hugging, and I barely noticed the pain in my back from her hands.

I grinned at the doctor. "A son," I said.

"Milt, Jr.," he said.

"Chip," I said.

"Skipper," he said.

"Buddy," I said.

"Bubba," he said.

Jean stood up. "If I hear any more of this male bonding I'm going to puke," she said, smiling from ear to ear.

I stood with her and shook hands with the doctor. "Thank you," I said. "Thank you so much."

"Don't thank me," he said. "The sex chromosome rests with the last one to have it—Jean. Thank her for your son."

Which is just what I planned on doing—privately and at home.

I drove into the parking lot of the sheriff's department a little after one in the afternoon. My staff resisted slapping me on the back, which I was grateful for, and I told them to hold everything while I made a phone call.

I went into my office and sat down with the phone on my lap and looked at my watch. At exactly 1:15 I dialed my sister's home number. This was politics. There were people who needed to know our baby was okay. Actually, everybody in town deserved to know that. But the politics was in the timing. Jean and I had decided that she'd call Melissa and I'd call Jewel exactly at the same time. That way, neither one could one-up the other or be mad at us about anything.

Jewel picked up on the second ring. "Hey, baby sister," I said.

"Well, hey yourself, bigness. What's going on?"

"Jean and I just got back from the doctor's office. We got the results of the amnio."

"Oh, Jesus, let me sit down." I heard Jewel pulling up a chair. "Okay. I'm ready."

"We got us a healthy baby boy brewing in there," I said, all grins.

My sister Jewel promptly burst into tears. As did Gladys when I told her, and even Dalton, when it was explained to him precisely what had been going on and what amniocentesis is, got a tear in his eye. Mike pumped my arm like it was an old spigot, grinning from ear to ear. It was a happy time. A happiness barely dampened by Mike Neils coming into my office an hour later.

"Thought I'd catch you up on what's been happening," Mike said, sitting down without even being asked to. I'da never sat down without the sheriff offering me a chair. I'd been thinking about offering Mike the chief deputy position, but with that uppity attitude, I just wasn't sure.

"I thought I already knew what's been going on. Your daily phone report?" I said, squinting at him.

"Well, Milt . . . Sheriff . . ." Mike said, squirming in his chair. "Ah. I didn't want you worrying none about things . . ."

"What the fuck's going on, Neils?"

Mike sighed. "It's that animal shelter thing, Sheriff. Two more mutilated cats were found. This time they were dumped on the steps of the bowling alley."

"Jesus," I leaned back hard in my chair, then remembered that wasn't something I wanted to be doing. I leaned forward, my mean look on my face. "From now on, Deputy, when I tell you to keep me informed, you damned well better keep me informed. Of everything. When it's happening. You understand me?"

Mike Neils sat up straighter. "Yes, sir," he said.

"When did this happen?"

"Two days ago, sir."

"Anything else happening at the shelter?"

"No, sir. Millard keeps calling, wanting to know if we know anything, but he says nothing else has been happening. They got extra security on at the shelter."

"I want you to take a ride by the high school around about the time school's out. You see anybody smoking cigarettes, you bring their butts in here."

"Sir?"

"There's an ordinance on the books say you can't smoke in public if you're underage. I'm gonna interrogate me some teenagers."

After Mike left, the phone rang. It was my lawyer, Bradley Watts.

"Well, hey, Bradley," I said. "Hear anything from Sheriff Marshall?"

"That's why I'm calling, Milt," Bradley said. "Marshall has decided not to charge you with anything."

I leaned back, then up again, real quick-like. "Well, thank the good Lord. And you, too, Bradley. I know you had a hand in this."

"The stupid s.o.b. doesn't know what he's doing, Milt. He wants to arrest somebody so bad his teeth ache, but there's nobody to arrest."

"Bill will find out what's going on."

"Don't bet on it," Watts said and hung up.

I wondered vaguely if I had any of that hefty retainer coming back to me in change, but somehow I figured I could chalk that one up to the cost of keeping one fairly well-fed ass out of lock-up.

I'd hardly put the phone back in the cradle when it rang again.

"Sheriff Kovak," I said. You know, I gotta admit, I liked saying that.

"Hey, pud face," Bill Williams said.

"Well, hey your ownself. What's going on?" I said.

"You ain't in jail, that's all that's going on over here."

"My lawyer just called said it's likely I ain't going to jail either," I said.

Bill snorted. "I tell you what, friend, having you in jail would make my life a helluva lot easier."

"Well, then, old buddy, I'll just haul my ass over there and get me a county suit. That's what you want?"

"I'd like it bunches. But I think between me and your lawyer, we done convinced the sheriff that you probably didn't do it."

I didn't thank him for the vote of confidence. It hardly seemed worth the effort. "Anything new on the investigation?"

"What do you know about Ulysses Strom, Gayla's daddy?"

I told him all I knew, including my theory that if he'da wanted to kill Wade, he woulda done it back when Wade first run off with his girl, twelve years before.

"Now, on the surface, that makes sense, Milt," Bill said. "But I got to thinking: Here this old tail-chaser shows up back home with Strom's baby girl in tow. Living with her bigger 'n nothing, right in daddy's own backyard, so to speak. Mighta got on his nerves. Mighta got him to thinking about that so-and-so messing with his little teenage baby girl back then and he just got so pissed off all over again that he decided to do something about it."

When Bill stopped for a breath, I said, "Well, it's better than nothing."

"That's what I thought," Bill said. "You wanna go with me to interview the old man?"

"How 'bout I set up something for tomorrow? I got some stuff of my own working here."

"Those animal mutilations?"

"Yep. Gonna roast me some teenagers this afternoon," I said.

"They're real good with a little *picante* sauce on the side," Bill said and hung up.

Around four P.M., Mike showed up with two nefarious teens in tow. He put one of 'em in one room with Dalton on guard so he wouldn't walk off with the plastic chairs, and put the other in the interrogation room. Then called me.

I walked in in my newly pressed and shiny sheriff's suit and strutted my stuff. The kid, Ronnie Jack Templette, was not impressed. I doubt if space aliens landing in the school cafeteria would impress Ronnie Jack. I didn't know Ronnie Jack or his kin as the family had moved to Longbranch the year before from Butte, Montana. Daddy was an oil rigger, is what I found out when Ronnie Jack lowered himself to answer a few questions. But I gotta admit, the look of the kid put me off some. He was wearing a Texas Rangers baseball cap turned around backward with lanky, no-color brown hair spilling out around the sides. In the middle of February, he was wearing an old Spuds McKenzie T-shirt with the sleeves ripped off and the armpits ripped down to his waist, showing off a hairless, skinny, dead-fish-white rib cage. His Levi's were baggy in the butt and splotched with bleach stains and his shoes were ancient running shoes with no socks, the heels and sides run over. If the boy was trying to make a statement, the statement seemed to be, "Look at me. I got dressed in the dark from a bag lady's cart." He had a weaselly face like a popular country singer, with an Adam's apple bigger than his head and oozing acne on his forehead and neck. Butte, Montana's loss was certainly our gain.

"So, what you do in Butte for fun, Ronnie Jack?" I asked.

"Nothing," he answered.

"Just sat on your butts day in and day out?"

He didn't respond.

"You ride around in cars any?"

"Yeah, some."

"You go anyplace in them cars?"

He shrugged.

"Did you have a drive-in or a restaurant ya'll liked to stop at occasionally?" I asked real friendly-like.

"Yeah, some," he said, shrugging.

"What was the name of the drive-in?" I asked.

He looked at me and snorted, then looked away.

"Didn't have no name?" I asked.

"Fuck if I know," he said. He reached into his shirt pocket and pulled out a cigarette and started to light it.

I swatted it from his hand, the cigarette landing on the floor. "Against city ordinance No. 43-210 for underaged fellas to smoke inside the city limits," I said.

Ronnie Jack smiled. "We ain't inside the city limits, Sheriff," he said.

Well, he had me on that one for sure. I smiled. "Let's just say you do it again, you might have yourself an accident, and I ain't talking about peeing your pants."

He snorted again but didn't reach for the cigarette pack.

"Now, Ronnie Jack, seems to me you been here a short time but you're in real thick with the in-crowd at school, right?"

He didn't feel like replying to that one.

"I got some questions. You ever hear about anybody playing

games at school like, oh, you know, fun stuff like calling up the devil, stuff like that?"

He laughed out loud. "Calling up the what?"

"The devil. Satan."

"Jesus H. Christ," he said, and laughed like an idiot.

I figured then was as good a time as any to release Ronnie Jack Templette, so I did, having Mike drive him back to the high school. Before he left, I told Mike when he got back to call Butte, Montana, and see if they had any trouble up there with Satanic-type rituals and if the locals knew anything about our young Templette boy. Then I set about interviewing teenager number two.

I was sorry to see this was Jared Blessing, whose daddy was the choir director at the Longbranch First Baptist. At least I had a handle on this one.

It was hard to see these two as running buddies. Jared was as different-looking from Ronnie Jack as two boys of the same age could be. Jared was small, no more than five foot six, small build, but with a muscular upper body. He was wearing a button-down checked shirt and khaki pants. His shoes were new high-dollar running shoes. His fingernails, I noticed, were clean and his face only had one pimple—about the size of Tulsa—on his left cheek.

Dalton brought him in and I just sat there and stared at him for about three minutes. Until he burst into tears and said, "Oh, Lord, Sheriff, don't tell my daddy I was smoking! Please!"

"You know there's a city ordinance?" I said.

"No, sir. No, sir, I didn't know that. I'm real sorry. If I'da known that, I never woulda . . . I mean . . . you gotta believe me, Sheriff . . ." he said through the tears and snot.

I sat back as gingerly as possible, looking stern, just like I was gonna look for my own boy when I caught him with his first cigarette, and said, "Stop the blubbering, Jared."

He sobbed a couple of times, sniffed, wiped his runny eyes and nose on a snowy white handkerchief he extracted from his back pocket, sighed real hard, and looked up at me with great big watery blue eyes. I'd prefer my own boy to have a little more gumption than that, but then, there ya go.

"Jared, you hear about the thefts at the animal shelter?" I asked.

The big eyes got bigger. "No, sir. I don't know anything about it. I swear."

"Seems a bunch of cats and dogs was stole. You hear about it?"

Jared started shaking his head so hard I thought he might lose some hair. "No, sir. I don't know anything! I swear!"

"We found some of the cats and one of the dogs," I said.

Jared leaned back and sighed. "Well, that's great, Sheriff, I'm real glad . . ."

"We found the dog in the ditch at the side of a road. Some of him, anyway. Some of him was on the road, some down the road, some, well, you get the picture."

Jared Blessing was turning a lovely shade of puce while I talked. I was beginning to fear for the linoleum.

"Oh, Jesus," he said. "Oh, sweet Jesus."

"Looks to me like we got us a cult right here in Longbranch. Little Satanic ritual kinda thing, Jared. What do you know about that kind of stuff?"

Jared sat up straight in his chair. "Sir, I'm a Baptist," he said.

"You know anybody at school into that kind of stuff?"

He shook his head hard. "No, sir! I swear! I never heard nobody talking about shit—stuff like that! I swear to Lord Jesus!"

"Any group at school doing stuff a little out of the ordinary? Piercing their noses or wearing clothes weirder than usual?"

"Ah, well, Lyla Miller has three holes in each ear. That what you mean?"

I shook my head. "Naw, I think that's more fashion than witchcraft. Anybody reading weird stuff?"

"You mean like Stephen King? Lots of people read him. He writes about stuff like that."

Jared was getting eager now. Ready to rat out his own mother if she didn't vote a straight Republican ticket. I leaned forward. I had me my very own spy and I knew it. "Jared," I said, quiet-like. "I need me some eyes and ears at the high school."

"Yes, sir," he said, leaning forward with me.

"You keep an eye out. You see anything—and I mean anything—that looks kinky, you holler, you hear?"

"Yes, sir," he said, "and, sir?"

"Yes, Jared?"

"You won't tell my daddy about my smoking?"

I held out my hand and he put his pack of Merit Light 100s in the palm. "Not this time," I said, crushing the pack in my hand, standing, and walking out the door. It was one of my better exists. Course, the kid was easy.

◀ 12 ▶

I released Jared Blessing, having Dalton drive him back to the high school, and went back to my office, looked up the number for Ulysses Strom's law office in Bishop, and dialed. His secretary answered and I made an appointment for me and Bill to drop by the next day. She wasn't real obliging, saying as how Mr. Strom had a full day in and out of court, but then I suggested, since he was gonna be in court so damned much, and since the courthouse is in Longbranch, that he just stop on by my office instead of us driving out to his. At that point she decided he had an opening at one P.M. and would be more than happy to see us at his office at that time. I smiled, said thank you, and hung up.

I was packing up to take off for the house when Mike Neils came into my office. He stood (he's learning) until I pointed at a chair, then sat down to report.

"Well, I called Butte like you said, Sheriff. Only, when I asked the guy who answered the phone for any info on Ronnie Jack Templette, he got real mean about it. Seems this deputy, August Lotz, is Ronnie Jack's mama's sister's boy . . ."

"You mean Ronnie Jack's cousin?" I asked.

Mike thought for a moment. "Well, yes, sir, I guess that would be right. Anyway, he said what are we harassing Ronnie Jack for and he's a good boy and what the fuck's going on . . . That part's a direct quote, Sheriff, you know I don't talk like that unless it's necessary."

I nodded. "I'm aware of that, Mike," I said.

"So, anyway. What you want me to do now?"

"Just hang tight, Mike. Call back in the morning and get you somebody who ain't actually related to Ronnie Jack and see if he's got any priors. Think you can do that, boy?"

Mike stood up. "Yes, sir," he said, not actually saluting but getting damned close to it. "No problem, sir."

He turned on his heel and left and I went home, pulling up to my house to see a parking lot. Jewel's wagon was there, as was Melissa's Miata and my brother-in-law Harmon's Cadillac. There was another car there I didn't recognize. A brand-new shiny Chrysler New Yorker.

Since the demise of my beloved '55, I was driving my unmarked squad car home, with the blessing of the county commissioners. I had a month to do that, then they expected me to have my own wheels again. Looking at that shiny New Yorker made me think maybe driving antique cars wasn't all it was cracked up to be.

Anyway, I got out of the squad car and headed for the door of my house, ready for the onslaught of well-wishers. Harmon had brought champagne and everybody except Jean and Jewel was drinking it. I discovered the owner of the Chrysler was Jean's secretary, Bette Raintree, and I couldn't help wondering how much the hospital paid her for her to be able to afford that classy New Yorker. Bette had consumed a little more of the champagne than she'd probably intended to. Enough anyway to jump up when I walked in the door and throw her arms around my neck and burst into tears.

"I'm so happy!" she wailed.

"Me, too," I said, patting her on the back and looking at my bride with a "what now" look on my face.

Jean maneuvered her crutches under her arms and came over to where Bette and I stood and led her secretary back to the sofa. Harmon punched me on the arm as I moved into the room and Melissa winked at me. My sister, I noticed, was sitting by herself sniffling. "Oh, if Mama were just alive to see this," she said, shaking her head over and over again.

I leaned over and kissed Jean where she sat comforting Bette Raintree and moved to the love seat next to my sister, sitting down and putting my arm around her shoulders.

"She'da been real happy, Jewel, about as happy as she was with you giving her three grandbabies."

Jewel shook her head. "No, even happier. Mama always said it was LaDonna's fault you couldn't have babies. She always knew that."

I looked at my sister. "She did? She never said anything to me."

Jewel looked at me and rolled her eyes. "Mama wouldn't. You know she didn't believe in interfering. But she never could stand LaDonna."

Well, this was certainly news to me. My mama, may she rest in peace, was a hell of a lady and, to her credit, neither me nor LaDonna ever knew how she felt. But I can't say as I blamed her. I never was too partial to LaDonna myself. She was a mean-spirited woman and, now that I look back on it, I think the main reason I married her in the first place was because she expected me to.

Well, we continued the evening with a lot of drinking and a lot of crying, with Jean and Jewel abstaining (from the drinking anyway—when you get Jewel to crying, it's near impossible to put a cork in it), and then me and Harmon set fire to the barbecue pit and roasted us some chickens and fed everybody. Jewel and Harmon's kids (including his two girls, who seemed nice enough to me, but, then again, I didn't have to live with them) showed up and we had us a party.

Melissa stayed on awhile to help clean up while I rocked Rebecca to sleep in Jean's rocking chair. It was good practice, both women insisted. It was almost eleven o'clock before Jean and I closed the door on the last of 'em. We went to bed and made love for the second time that day, slow and easy, just like the rest of our life together was gonna be. I fell asleep a happy man.

The next morning, after holding my bride for about twenty minutes and just looking into the depths of those hazel eyes, I called Bill Williams and told him of our appointed time with Ulysses Strom. He said okay and I left the house for the sheriff's department, stopping on my way at the Longbranch Memorial Hospital to have a talk with Dr. Jim.

He was sitting at his desk, feet up on the top of it, reading a copy of *People* magazine when I walked in the door.

"I guess when you ain't busy the county can breathe a sigh of relief," I said.

"You gonna get them dead animals outta my freezer?" he asked, not looking up from his article about the man who invented bungee jumping.

I pulled up a straight-back chair and sat down across from him at his desk. "Can you tell me any more about what's going on with them animals, Dr. Jim?"

He glanced up at me, pushing his reading glasses down to the tip of his nose. "They're dead. Just like they was the last time you asked."

"The last bunch that Mike Neils brought you—were they mutilated the same way? Ritual-like?"

"Sloppy but ritualistic. Same kinda mutilation. Same kinda torture. You find this bunch, Milton, you let me do a little autopsying on 'em before you jail 'em, okay? Maybe take their brains out, see what makes 'em tick."

I stood up and patted his desk. "I'll surely think on it, Dr. Jim," I said, and took my leave.

I drove over to the animal shelter and went into Millard Running Deer's office.

He looked up as I walked in. "You find them assholes yet, Milt?"

I shook my head and sat down in one of his visitor's chairs. "Not yet, Millard. Ain't got nothing to go on. But we're still plowing through."

"It's sick, Milt. That's what it is."

"I know. You got any disgruntled employees around here?"

Millard shook his head. "I'm the only employee, Milt. The rest of 'em's all volunteers."

I shook my head. This one might be the death of me, I was feeling. 'Cause I didn't have a clue in hell as to what was going on. Hopefully, my high school spy would turn up something. "Change of subject," I said to Millard.

"Okay."

"You Maria Running Deer's daddy?"

Millard sat up straight. "Yeah. Something wrong?"

I leaned back gingerly. "Naw. Nothing like that. I just saw her when I was picking up a little friend of mine at Opal Allen's the other day. Rebecca Robinson? She's sorta my adopted granddaughter."

Millard nodded his head. "Seems to me that's one of the names of the other little girls that didn't get invited to Mindy Reynolds' birthday party."

"Yeah, that's right. Rebecca's mama and me been thinking it

would be nice if the girls could have their own party. I got a friend with a horse ranch said he'd be proud as punch to have the girls go out there and party with some gentle horses. You up for that?"

Millard nodded. "Beats the hell out of my wife's idea," he said.

"What's that?" I asked.

"She wanted me to save up all the dog and cat crap from around here and go dump it in the Reynolds' living room the morning of the party," Millard said, laughing. "Can you beat that? And I thought she was such a sweet woman when I married her."

"You don't never mess with a she-animal's cub," I said.

"Ain't it the truth?" He shook his head again. "You know, when we moved to Longbranch, we thought that kinda stuff was behind us, Milt. Then there was that Patriots for a Free America bullshit last year, and now this."

"You know what they say, Millard," I said. "You can lead a horse to water but you can't beat him with a coat hanger."

"Do they say that, Milt?" he asked.

"I don't know, but they should."

With that, I left and headed back to the office.

Mike was fidgeting like crazy when I walked in the office. Seeing me, he jumped up and rushed to follow me into my office. He stood, prancing back and forth on his feet, like a little boy trying not to pee in his pants, while I hung up my uniform jacket and sat down at my desk. I pointed at the chair in front of the desk and Mike sat, squirming all the while, then said, "About Butte, Milt? Sheriff?"

"What about Butte, Mike?"

"I talked to somebody who's not related to Ronnie Jack Templette," he said and grinned.

"Good for you," I said, and waited.

"The head of the juvie unit there. Seems Ronnie Jack's had a few run-ins, but nothing like this business. DUI last year and a D and D about two weeks before they moved on. But that's all."

"Keep an eye on him," I said. "Talk to his folks and, if he's got brothers and sisters, talk to them. See how he treats the family dog."

Mike stood up. "Sure thing, Milt."

Mike left the office and, while I was thinking on it, I called the county electric utility department and told 'em I thought there might be a wiring problem over at the Reynolds RV Sales and Service. They said they'd send an inspector out right away to check on that. Then I called the water department and told 'em I'd smelled raw sewage around Clifford and Maxine Reynolds' house out in Bishop. Then I sat back and smiled the smile of a mean but satisfied man.

I took lunch at the Longbranch, accustomed now to having Loretta Dubjek wait on me rather than Glenda Sue. I still didn't sit in Glenda Sue's old section, as it didn't seem to be the right thing to do, somehow. I was able to get back to eating chicken-fried steak, so that's what I had for lunch. Then I drove to Bishop to Ulysses Strom's office to meet Bill Williams to sit in on the interrogation.

Bill was sitting in his squad car waiting for me when I drove up. He got out and I offered my hand to shake. To give the boy credit, he didn't even flinch, just shook it like I wasn't his very best murder suspect.

"How you gonna handle this old boy?" I asked him.

Bill shrugged. "This is your jurisdiction, Milt, thought I'd let you take the lead."

"Yeah, but this here is your investigation, Bill. I'm just along to make it official."

"Yeah," he said, "but you know Ulysses Strom and I don't.

Besides, you knew the deceased and I barely even met the man. See?"

"Jeez Louise," I said. "You gonna make me do all the work, aren't you, Bill?"

Bill grinned. "Hell, Milt," he said, "you won't let me lock you up."

I shook my head and led him into Ulysses Strom's building. The secretary, a mean-mouthed woman about my age, told us to sit and we did. I looked around the office. It wasn't exactly up to Bradley Watts's standards. Everything was new and cheap. The carpet was regulation indoor-outdoor gray. The walls were painted half-green and half-gray. The chairs were upholstered in a tweedy green that didn't quite match the green of the walls. The pictures on the walls were enlarged photographs of flowers. All in all, I'd take Bradley Watts's office any day of the week.

After about ten minutes, Ulysses Strom opened his office door and strode toward us. He was still a big man, but a lot of the big was running to fat. His jowls hung down like a basset hound's and the material of his shirt stretched against the belly. I hadn't seen Ulysses Strom in twelve years. Not since the scene in the sheriff's office when Wade and Gayla first run off.

Strom flashed a big smile and stuck his hand at me, so I shook it. As did Bill when it came his turn. Then Strom said, "Well, boys, why don't ya'll come on in my office and sit down? May Ella, you wanta get us some coffee? You boys want some coffee?"

He shut the door on May Ella before she ever heard whether we wanted some or not, but as she never showed up with any, I guess that was as it should be. Bill and I sat down on the two leatherette chairs in front of Strom's desk while he took the big one behind the desk. As was his right. It was his desk.

"Now," he said, still smiling, "what can I do for you boys?"

"We need to talk some about old Wade's murder, Mr. Strom," I said, sitting sincere-like.

Strom stopped smiling and shook his head sadly. "That was something, wadn't it? I want you boys to know my little girl's taking it real hard."

"Yes, sir," I said, "I was the one had to take her over to identify the body."

He shook his head some more. "Wish you'da come got me, boy," he said. "I hate for my girl to haveta done that."

"Yes, sir, but we have to have the nearest kin and that would be his wife, Mr. Strom."

Strom nodded his head. "I understand. I understand. But I'm her daddy, and," he smiled, "I still wanna protect her, ya know? Even if she is a grown-up woman."

I smiled back. "That's only natural, Mr. Strom."

He leaned back in his chair. "Okay, boys, what can I do for you?"

"Well," I said, "we was wondering if you mighta seen Wade that morning?"

He shook his head. "No, boy. I hadn't seen Wade for about a week before the . . . well, before it happened."

"You hear about anybody unhappy with Wade?" I asked him.

"Ah, hell, Milt, you knew Wade better than me! He was a good ol' boy. Everybody loved Wade."

"I understand you didn't take to him too well," Bill said, opening his mouth for the first time and putting his foot right in it.

"Son?" Strom asked, looking hard at Bill.

"Being as how your little girl was only sixteen when she run off with Wade. What was he then, Milt? Thirty, thirty-five?"

"Thirty-seven," I answered.

"Whew," Bill said, shaking his head. "I got me a girl about that age right now, Mr. Strom. I know how I'd feel if some grown man was messing with my little girl."

Strom laughed and shook his head. "Son, I was pissed to beat the band when he run off with Gayla. I'll admit that. That girl had a future. She coulda twirled baton at O.U. Instead, she run off with a no-account deputy sheriff." He looked at both of us. "No offense meant," he added.

"Add to that," I said, "that they lied to you about her being pregnant. I would think—"

Strom's face got stormy. "Who told you that, boy? Gayla was pregnant, all right. But she lost the baby. She was all messed up inside, the doctor said, and they had to give her a total hysterectomy and she was shy of seventeen years." He shook his head. "Liketa broke my wife's heart. Gayla's our only child, ya know. Now we won't never have any grandbabies."

I sat back, oblivious of the dull pain in my back. "I'm sorry, Mr. Strom. I didn't know that. There just never was any baby, so I just thought—"

"That'll teach you to think twice, boy." He looked at Bill. "So you think 'cause Wade run off with my baby girl that I waited twelve years till he gets close enough to me, then I killed his butt?"

Bill said, "It's a thought, Mr. Strom."

"Well, it's a stupid thought. That boy was good to my little girl. He helped her through the roughest time in her life, when she lost the baby and the chance to ever have any more. He took off from work and he stayed with her, night and day." Strom sat back and glared at us. "I'm a big enough man to admit when I been wrong, and I admitted that to Wade Moon twelve years ago." He stood up. "Now, if that's all, boys, I gotta be in court in half an hour and I got some briefs to go over. So . . ." He pointed at the door.

Me and Bill could take a hint.

◀ 13 ▶

We stopped by Bernie's Chat and Chew for a cup of coffee and a piece of pie before heading back to work. I had pecan and Bill had apple with vanilla ice cream. It looked so good I wished I'd ordered that instead of the pecan.

"Well, whatja think?" I asked Bill.

He shrugged. "He's a lawyer. Lawyers are born liars."

"Well, that's true enough," I said, "but you think he's lying now?"

He shrugged again. "Who can tell with a lawyer?"

I nodded my head in agreement. Then I said, "Way I look at it, we got Ulysses Strom, his daughter Gayla, and both the other Moon women, Edna Earle and Lonnette. And," I grinned, "of course, me. Anybody else come to mind?"

"What about the other daughter?"

"Tula? She's ain't but twelve years old!"

"Been known to happen," Bill insisted.

"You don't know this girl. 'Sides, why? Why any of 'em?"

Bill did everything but lick the bottom of his pie plate, sat back, and sipped his coffee. "Well, that's something we obviously don't know yet, Milt. If we were to figure out the why, I think we'd figure out the who."

We both sipped at our coffee then Bill said, "What about

Strom's wife? Could she be harboring a grudge against Wade 'cause her baby can't have no grandchildren?"

I shrugged. "What about when he was working with you?" Bill asked. "He ever put anybody away who might be obliged to hold a grudge?"

I thought about it. We had wrecks on the highway, misdemeanor murders at the Sidewinder Lounge, wife beatings, child beatings, and a theft or two, but not much grudgematch-type stuff. I shook my head. "I can't think of a damned thing, Bill."

"Well, the upshot of all this is, Milt, that boy's still dead. And somebody had to kill him. You go with me to talk to the ex-wife tomorrow?"

I sighed. "Bill, you know I got my own county to run."

"These people are in your county, Milt. I can't help it if they came over to my county to do their dirty work."

"Well, tell you what, Bill," I said standing and grabbing the check before he could, "tomorrow's Saturday and I got me a new wife. How 'bout we make it Monday?"

Bill stood and grinned. "Boy, you too old to be doing it all day long."

"Monday," I said, ignoring his comment.

"Okay," he said, "Monday. You set it up?"

"No sweat," I said, paid the bill and took my leave.

Jean and I spent Friday evening having supper with Jewel and Harmon and the kids, then drove on back to Mountain Falls Road, pulling up to our place at about ten. We went in and Jean turned the light on in the living room.

"I don't like the way the living room's arranged," she said.

I kept my sighing silent, but I knew it was starting up again. All because Jewel made a little comment at the dinner table. An innocent little comment. Just, "I wished I'd known it was a boy when I did the nursery, I would have made the walls blue instead of yellow."

Jean had said hardly a word after that. I figured for a psychiatrist, she should recognize repressed hostility when it was hitting her like a ton of cow paddies. I figured if she had a problem with Jewel Anne, she should fix it. But then again, with hormones racing through her like Secretariat in a paddock of mares in heat, I wasn't about to do my figuring out loud.

"Well, we can do that tomorrow," I said, referring to rearranging the living room. "We got us a whole Saturday to do whatever we want."

"I have to work," she said, moving with her crutches up the two steps to the foyer and into the kitchen. I turned the living room light off and followed her.

"Work? You gotta work?" I said.

"Yes," she said, the "yes" very definite and very nasty. "I'm a professional psychiatrist. We don't work nine to five. I'm responsible for a ten-bed unit at the hospital. I have eight of those beds filled. I'm the only psychiatrist on duty. Ever. Is that a problem for you?"

"Well, no, honey, of course not—"

"Because if it's a problem for you, Milt, I'll be happy to quit. Stay home and be a happy little homebody like your precious sister."

I opened the door to the bedroom, went in, and closed it behind me. Locking the lock. Two could play this game. And I could be just as childish as the next guy. Even if the next guy was my pregnant wife.

I sat down on the bed, listening to the skitter sounds of her crutches on the linoleum as she moved away from the bedroom door. I heard the slam of a chair against the table. I heard the slam of a cabinet door. I heard the slam of the refrigerator door. Then I heard her pick up the phone extension in the kitchen.

Then I heard, "Melissa? . . . This is Jean . . . I need some place to sleep tonight . . ."

I opened the bedroom door.

"You wanna hang up now?" I asked.

"Never mind. I'll call you later," Jean said into the phone, then hung up, keeping her back to me, staring at the blank wall in front of her.

"Look," I said, "Jewel's my sister and I love her. But she done something that hurt you. You need to deal with that or it'll fester and you two will have a mad on for the rest of our lives. I don't wanna have that. I hate family squabbles. Now, if you don't wanna deal with Jewel, then I will. But this here is gonna be dealt with, Jean, one way or the other."

"Are you through?" she said, her back still to me.

"Well, yeah, I guess I am," I said, my temper showing.

She turned to face me. "I don't need you fighting my battles for me," she said, her mouth set hard.

"Then fight your own goddamn battles, woman!"

"Don't call me woman!"

I sighed. "Oh, for Christ's sake. We're gonna have a fight, aren't we? You are bound and determined we're gonna have a fight."

"Did I start this?" Jean yelled.

"Yes, ma'am, I think you did," I said, keeping my temper admirably.

"Oh, no! I didn't start this! Your fucking sister started this!"

I put my hand on her arm in a gentle manner. "Honey, I think your hormones are a little out of whack—"

She pulled her arm away. "Don't you talk to me about hormones! I'm an MD, you jerk!"

"Jean, calm down, honey—"

"Don't you tell me to calm down! I am as calm as I need to be at the moment! I am dealing here with the obvious products of a dysfunctional family—"

"Who you calling a dysfunctional family?" I said.

"Your sister's meddling is inbred, Milton. That much is obvious," she said, her voice lower now, but hard. "Her need to be the constant center of attention stems from an obvious delusion of abandonment as a young child—"

"Whoa, lady!" I said. "You know nothing about Jewel or me as children. Keep your snotty psychiatric nose out of it!"

Jean laughed mirthlessly. "Well. I guess that says it all, doesn't it?"

"What's that supposed to mean?"

"Do you want a divorce?" she asked, coming from outta left field.

"No, I don't want a divorce—"

"Because that would be quite all right with me. I realize I'll be the first one in my family to ever get a divorce, but then again, I'm the first in my family to ever marry someone who had already *been* divorced—"

"Jean—"

"What?"

I walked up to her and put my hand on her face, cradling her cheek in my palm. "Woman, you're gonna be the death of me."

She sighed. "I'm getting a little weird, Milt," she said, looking down at her feet. "I hear what I'm saying and I know I'm saying it. And I want to say it." She looked up at me. "Even when I know it's stupid."

"I love you," I said.

She sighed again. "I love you, too."

"Come on," I said, "let's go to bed."

I held her in my arms until she fell asleep. Somewhere around three A.M., she woke me up, muttering in her sleep. I sat up and listened. She was saying "Goddamn bitch" over and over, and I was pretty sure I was related to the bitch she was referring to.

Jean got up at seven to get ready to go to the hospital. I got up with her. The older I get the harder I find it to sleep in on a Saturday.

"So, you gonna have to work all day?" I asked.

"Probably. Did you have something you wanted to do today?" she asked, sweet as pie.

"Well, I was thinking of going car shopping," I said.

"Yuck," she said, pulling a carton of blueberry yogurt out of the door of the refrigerator. "I hate car shopping. Can't you get someone else to go with you?"

I couldn't imagine somebody who didn't like to look at cars, but then again, like I've always said, women are weird creatures.

"Well," I said, "maybe I'll call Emmett."

"That's a good idea. You know what you want?"

"I sure liked the looks of that Chrysler New Yorker Bette Raintree was driving the other night. How can she afford a car like that?"

"Her husband's a supervisor out at the refinery. As I understand it, he's been there almost twenty years and makes probably more money than I do."

"Oh. You think them New Yorkers are expensive?"

Jean shrugged. "Comparable to a Cadillac or a Lincoln," she said, finishing up the yogurt and grabbing her purse. She leaned over to where I sat at the kitchen table and kissed me. "I gotta go, babe. See you later this afternoon. Call me when you get back."

And with that she was gone. Little Mary Sunshine. All peaches and cream. I swear to God, not one of those men at the bachelor party had pregnancy as rough as I was having it. And that's the goddamn truth.

I piddled around the house for a while, trying to stay out of Evinrude's way. He'd taken to swiping at me with his claws out whenever I was within reach. Retribution can be a bitch, they say. Around nine, I called Emmett Hopkins, chief of police of Longbranch and my old friend, at home.

"Hey, Emmett," I said after his hello. "This is Milt."

"Well, hey yourself. How's married life treating you?"

"Don't even ask."

"It's just damn lucky pregnant women look so damn good or they'd never live through it," Emmett said, laughing.

I'd heard men say that before but I couldn't see it. Jean wasn't swole up yet, so I didn't know how she'd look, but I remember seeing lots of women pregnant and I never once thought they glowed. Course, none of 'em was ever carrying my child before either.

"Look, Emmett," I said, "you hear about the '55?"

"Jesus, yes. And Milt, I cried. I want you to know, man, I just cried."

"Well, thank you, Emmett, I appreciate that. But now I gotta find me another car. I was wondering if you'd like to drive up the Tulsa Highway to that Chrysler dealership? I wanna look at one of them New Yorkers."

"Whew, boy, you get a raise?"

I grinned. "Got me a rich wife."

I drove the squad car to Emmett's house in Longbranch to pick him up, armed with my checkbook, in which I'd just deposited the seven thousand dollars the insurance had coughed up. Up until I'd had the new paint job on the '55, I'd carried liability only. Then I got to talking to my insurance man and he'd said what I had there was a antique. I should insure it as an antique. But then he said I couldn't drive it to work every day. So we settled on how many days a year I could drive it to work and still have it insured as "parade value," which is what they call it, and then I fudged it just a bit, but that's just between you and me. Then I had it appraised and the dealer said he'd give me seven thou for it right there on the spot. Considering what I'd spent on it original and what I'd put into it, that was a nice piece of change, but I never would have sold the '55. But now I figured no matter how much them New Yorkers cost, seven thou would take a nice little bite out of what I had to finance.

Emmett lived in an older house, built in the twenties with a wide front porch and gables on the second floor. Lots of gingerbread around the eaves. The yard was winter-trimmed, the sidewalks edged. In the summer, the yard was ablaze with flowers and foliage, everything that would grow in our part of the country and even some that most said wouldn't.

Emmett had turned into a fine gardener and sometimes shared the bounty of his backyard vegetable garden with me—vine-ripened tomatoes, bell peppers big as a softball, and cucumbers the size of a male porn star. Five years back, Emmett had the scruffiest yard in Longbranch. Full of bicycles, basketball hoops, kids' toys, and bald spots in the yard where games of touch football were played. But that was before J.R. died of leukemia.

Shirley Beth, Emmett's wife, was standing at the living room window, looking out. I waved but she didn't wave back. Probably didn't see me. Shirley Beth didn't see much of anything anymore. Ever since their boy died, Shirley Beth had took to drinking. She was a very quiet, ladylike drunk. Never any noise out of Shirley Beth.

I looked at her standing there. A ghost of her former self. She'd always been quiet. A ladylike woman, as my mama used to say. But pretty. Pretty as a picture. Up until the day they told her J.R., her boy, had leukemia. The shriveling started then and picked up speed a year later when the boy died. She wasn't pretty anymore. She wasn't anything anymore. Just a ghost lady standing at a window waiting. For what, nobody, including Shirley Beth, seemed to know.

Emmett came out the front door at my second horn honk and I got out of the squad car. "Can we take your car?" I asked him. "The county's been nice enough to let me use this thing, but they probably wouldn't look real kindly on me taking it out of the county."

"No problem," Emmett said, leading me up the driveway to his private car. A brand-new Toyota. I got in and the seat belt slammed itself against me when he started up the engine.

"Jesus," I said.

Emmett laughed. "Been a long time since you been in anything newer or fancier than a squad car, huh, Milt?"

"You get good mileage on this thing?"

"Great," he said, backing out of the driveway. "Thirty in town, forty on the highway."

"Damn," I said. "But this is Japanese, right?"

"Sure it's Japanese. It's a Toyota. You got something against the Japanese?"

"Well, no. But my daddy always said buy American."

Emmett pulled into traffic on Highway 5 heading for the Tulsa Highway and said, "So did mine. But then again, he never got forty miles to the gallon."

The Chrysler dealership was halfway between Longbranch and Tulsa, about an hour's drive. We talked for a while, about my cases, his cases, my new wife, my sister—anything and everything but the one subject we never did more than brush on—his wife, Shirley Beth. I always asked after her, he always said "she's fine" and that was the end of that.

I guess it could be said that Emmett Hopkins was my best friend. I'd known him since the sheriff's department was housed at the county courthouse—before we moved into our new building a few years back—when we were on the first floor to the left of the stairway and the city police were on the first floor to the right of the stairway.

We used to go out to lunch together, mostly after Wade Moon left and I needed a new friend. Last year he proved his friendship to me—taking me on as a deputy when I'd lost my county shield, helping me find Rebecca. Earlier on, I was the only person—save one—who knew about the one and only time he messed around on his wife. And I was the person he got drunk with on the night he found out J.R. had leukemia. But we didn't talk about Shirley Beth. That was an unwritten law. And I respected that.

"So who you think tried to blow your ass to kingdom come?" Emmett asked.

"Well, now, Emmett. I'm not sure. I figure it's got to have something to do with either that animal mess we got brewing here or the Wade Moon killing. More likely the Wade Moon killing since that shows a definite homicidal tendency, don'tcha think? I mean, the animal mutilations are pretty awful, but that's cats and dogs and not people, right?"

"Unless they've moved up the food chain a little bit," Emmett said.

"But while I was down, they found more animals. Don't make sense," I argued.

"Like mutilating animals in the first place makes sense, Milt?"

"You gotta think like a criminal mind, Emmett," I said. "It don't make sense to practice on cats and dogs first and then move on to humans, only to go back to cats and dogs."

"Yeah, but they blew it on the humans, Milt. You're still here."

"Hm," I said. The boy had a point. I wasn't crazy about it, but he had a point. "You're saying then that since they didn't kill me they had to go back to practicing on the animals and they're gonna try it again?"

"Well . . . yeah, that's a distinct possibility."

We were silent the twenty minutes more it took to get to the car store. As we pulled in, admiring the signs that said Chrysler, Jeep, GMC Trucks, and Oklahoma Outlet for Rolls-Royce, Emmett said, "Wish I'd thought to tell you to wear your uniform."

"Why's that?" I asked, trying to figure out how to undo my seat belt.

Emmett reached across me and hit the appropriate button. " 'Cause you could get yourself a deal. Anyway, introduce yourself as the sheriff of Prophesy County. That way, the salesman will think that when the time comes, if he gives you a good deal, he'll have an in with the county when they go to buy new cars."

"Is that honest?" I asked.

Emmett just looked at me, got out of the car, and started walking. We went up entirely too many steps to the door of the showroom. It was a huge dealership that advertised not only on the Tulsa stations but on other Oklahoma stations as well, saying as how they were out in the sticks, people taking the effort could get themselves a real deal. I took one look at the sticker price on that New Yorker and, after choking slightly, wondered how much more they could possibly ask for in the city.

Then I turned my head slightly—and fell in love. It was big, boxy, and metallic green. It had wood trim. And a roof rack. It sat right outside the big window and I found myself gravitating to it. I went outside and stared at it. I opened the door. It had a lovely sound as it opened. The inside was dark tan.

"This is the Jeep Briarwood," a voice behind me said. "Hunter green with dark sand leather interior. This one was ordered special and the guy never picked it up. Fully loaded. AM/FM cassette with Dolby. Power windows and door locks. Security system. Sunroof."

I shut the door, enjoying the solid sound it made. I moved to the hood. The man who had followed me out, the man who had been speaking, opened the car door, reached inside, and popped the hood up.

"Two-point-five-liter with multipoint fuel injection. One hundred and ninety horsepower."

I walked around the car, inspecting the tires, admiring the wood trim.

"And, of course, four-wheel drive and I'll throw in the winch that's already installed for the former buyer. What are you trading, friend?"

It took a strength of iron not to just hand him my checkbook.

"My car was totaled," I said.

"That's a shame. Real sorry to hear that." He opened the driver's-side door. "Want to take it for a spin?"

I moved awkwardly toward it, feeling like a teenager on his first date. I'd never even been in a brand-new car before. Not a spanking-new still-on-the-lot car. The '55 had been my first and only car. When LaDonna and I had been married, whatever car she drove had come from her brother's used car lot. He always gave her one at cost, so we never even went shopping.

I sat there and touched the upholstery. Leather. Smelled like leather. Wood-grain dash. Driver's-side airbag. Finally, I said, "*This* is a Jeep?"

The salesman got in the passenger side and grinned. "Car doesn't have to be ugly to be a mother, right, my friend?" He held out his hand. "Jackie Davidson. And you're?"

"Milt Kovak. Sheriff of Prophesy County," I added, remembering what Emmett had said.

I took a good look at Jackie Davidson. Brown polyester pants and a beige western-cut shirt with a silver and turquoise string tie. Endangered-species cowboy boots and a hundred-dollar silver-and-turquoise belt buckle. Half-carat diamond on his pinkie and a thick gold bracelet watchband.

"Well, now," he said, smiling, "Sheriff, why don't you start her up? Listen to her purr. Put you to sleep she's so gentle."

I turned the key, put the five-speed transmission into first gear, and moved slowly around the lot while Jackie Davidson picked his teeth with a gold toothpick.

At a little after four in the afternoon, I pulled into my driveway on Mountain Falls Road in a brand-new Jeep Briarwood. I had a car note for the first time in my life—a little less a month than I woulda paid for a New Yorker, but still a chunk of change, but God help me, it was pretty.

I honked the horn and Jean came to the door, leaning on her crutches. I got out and stood proudly at the driver's door of my Jeep. "Lookee what I got!" I said, beaming.

She walked out the door and up to the car, walking slowly around it. Leaning on her crutches for support, she looked in the driver's door. "Five-speed transmission?" she asked.

"Yeah," I said.

"How am I supposed to drive that?" she demanded.

I bristled. "About as well as you drove the three-speed in my '55."

Jean's car, a ten-year-old Buick, had special hand instruments so she could drive it. "So I don't get to drive this?"

"You want me to take it back? Have hand instruments added?"

She sighed. "No, of course not." She leaned over and kissed me. "It's just a mixture of hormones and jealousy. I've always wanted a Jeep."

I walked her around and opened the passenger-side door.

"Wanna get in and go for a spin? We can try going up and down the side of the mountain, if you wanna."

Jean got in and slammed the door. "How about we stick to the roads for a while?" she said.

◀ 14 ▶

Monday morning I called Edna Earle Moon before I left the house, making plans for me and Bill to meet with her sometime that day. She said we could meet her at the Bishop Elementary around 1:30, after the two lunch periods were over, or at her trailer house around three. I opted for the school, not wanting to possibly run into little Tula at the house. And, maybe, partly, so as not to have to look at Lonnette Moon. The girl spooked me and I'm the first to admit it.

I called Bill, told him about the meeting with Edna Earle, and then drove my brand-new Jeep to the station. I pulled into my parking place, smack dab next to the back door (one of the perks of being sheriff—although it still had Elberry's name on the space), and honked the horn. Then got out and stood proudly next to the car while my employees came out the back door to have a look.

And, I wanna tell you, it was snazzy. The dark green metallic exterior and the dark sand interior, the roof rack, the winch, the sunroof. All of it. Mike and Dalton oohed and aahed while Gladys looked on, said, "You got a new car?," shrugged and walked back inside. Women just don't know what's important.

I bent down to show Mike how the winch worked when the shot rang out. Hitting Dalton Pettigrew high on the shoulder.

The strength of the blast threw Dalton against the Jeep, slamming his head against the driver's door. Taking him down like a ton and a half of bricks.

Mike and I both drew our weapons, grabbing Dalton and dragging him to the safe side of the Jeep. We peeked around the taillight of the car, our guns at the ready, and all I could think of was, "Lord, don't let 'em put any holes in my Jeep!" Then, of course, I felt real bad about that.

Gladys stuck her head out the door. "Sheriff—"

"Get back inside!" I yelled. "Get an ambulance and call for backup!"

Within minutes, two city patrol cars, my two night deputies—A.B. Tate and Jasmine Bodine—and a highway patrol car pulled into the parking lot. The ambulance was just a few seconds behind them. Not another shot had been fired. Whoever he was, wherever he'd come from, he was gone now. And the asphalt parking lot was quiet, except for the shallow breathing of Dalton laying in a pool of his own blood, and all the yammering coming from the assorted law personnel present.

We got Dalton to the hospital, me in the back of the ambulance with him, holding his hand. He never did come to in the ambulance, or on the way to surgery. They had him in the operating room by nine A.M. and I was sitting in the waiting room with Mike, Gladys, Jean, and Jasmine, who was crying fit to beat the band. Dalton's mama was also there, a little woman still in her housedress and apron, although she'd put on her Sunday-go-to-meeting coat and had her Bible in her hands. She sat alone, praying and mumbling to herself.

A little before noon, the doctor came out. Seeing Jean, he went up to her first. "Which is family?" he asked her.

Jean pointed to Mrs. Pettigrew, sitting by herself.

"Introduce me," he said, taking Jean's arm. The doctor led her over to Dalton's mama.

Jean said, "Mrs. Pettigrew?" Leaning as much forward as she could on her crutches, she touched the older woman's shoulder. "Mrs. Pettigrew, this is Dr. Sawyer. He would like to speak with you about Dalton."

The old lady slowly stood up, her Bible clutched to her bosom. "Yes, sir?" she said.

The doctor smiled. "He's gonna be fine, ma'am," he said.

Mrs. Pettigrew said, "Praise Jesus!" and kissed the doctor's hand.

Dr. Sawyer motioned to a nurse nearby and had her take Mrs. Pettigrew to Dalton's bedside.

I moved in. "Doctor," I said, "I'm the sheriff, Dalton's boss."

"My husband," Jean said.

Which was obviously more impressive because his frown at my intrusion turned to a smile and he shook my hand. "Well, hey, nice to meet you."

"Thank you. How is he, doctor?"

"He's going to need physical therapy. The bullet did a lot of damage once it got inside. Tore a lot of cartilage and tendons. Is he right-handed or left-handed?"

"Right," I answered.

"Good. He won't be using the left for six months to a year."

I went with the whole gang to the hospital cafeteria where we all had a bite to eat, then went back up before leaving to check on Dalton. They let me in to see him.

And a pitiful sight it was. His mama was sitting at his bedside, reading Scripture, and Dalton lay like a great big old slug in the bed, his face white, his shoulder bandaged and his arm in a sling across his chest.

"Hey, Dalton," I said.

"Hey, Sheriff, I'm real sorry!"

I sat down in a chair on the opposite side of the bed from his mama and patted his good hand. "Boy, what you got to be sorry about? Not your fault some asshole—" I looked at Mrs. Pettigrew, who had turned an incredible shade of red, and said, "Excuse me, ma'am. Dalton, it ain't your fault. You just do what the doctors say and get better. I need you!"

We said our goodbyes, me promising to come back and see him later that afternoon, and I headed out to Bishop to meet with Bill Williams and interview Edna Earle Moon.

Sometimes I think not only are they serving the same types of food in the school systems today as they did when I was a kid, but maybe actually the same goddamn food. The smell was so strong a memory-inducer that I almost expected to see Jimmy Ralph Comstock sticking stewed okra up his nose to impress the girls.

Edna Earle was behind the serving counter cleaning up when Bill and I came into the cafeteria. She spoke to one of the women and then moved around the counter into the cafeteria proper, taking a seat at one of the tables that had not yet been put away and folding her hands in front of her on the tabletop. She was wearing a white smock over her housedress, tiny feet in tennis shoes crossed daintily under her chair.

"Sheriff," she said as Bill and I lowered our respective bulks onto the small little plastic stools. They were attached to the tables by a large metal crosspiece, as if the school board was saying "You just can't trust children."

I introduced Bill to Edna Earle, who nodded at him, not offering her hand because women in her day didn't do that.

"Miz Moon," Bill said, "I hate to bother you with this, but we got to get as much information as we can about Wade Moon's movements the morning of his death."

"Yes, sir," Edna Earle said.

"Did you see him that morning?"

"No, sir," Edna Earle said.

"When was the last time you seen Wade, Miz Moon?"

Edna Earle thought for a moment. "The night before. He come by to see Tula."

"Him and Tula get along okay?"

"Yes, sir," Edna Earle said.

"Tula happy to have her daddy back in town?" Bill asked.

Edna Earle thought on that one for a moment. "I suppose so, yes, sir," she said.

"She ever say anything?"

"Not that I recall."

"What about your other daughter?" Bill asked.

"Lonnette?"

"Yes, ma'am?"

"What about her, sir?" Edna Earle asked.

"She see a lot of Wade since he been back?"

"Some."

"She say anything about that?" Bill asked.

"Not that I recall," Edna Earle answered.

Bill sighed and I almost felt sorry for him, but I knew this interview was going to go nowhere when he'd suggested it and I'd tried to tell him so. Though obviously not hard enough.

"Miz Moon," I said.

She looked at me. "Yes, Sheriff?"

"You know anybody who'd wanna kill Wade?" I asked.

"No, sir," she answered.

Bill stood up. "Well, thank you for your time, Miz Moon," he said, and I followed him out the door to his squad car.

"Lord God almighty!" Bill said. "That woman talks less than any woman I ever heard of! It ain't natural!"

"She's a bit closemouthed," I admitted.

"Now what?" Bill said.

I shrugged. "Your investigation," I said.

"Then let's go out to that trailer house. Lonnette Moon'd be there, right?"

I shivered inside. "Now, Bill, I don't think—"

"You know the way, right? I'll follow you."

I sighed, shrugged, and got in my squad car to head out to Holiday Hell.

Lonnette Moon answered on our first knock. She pulled the trailer door open and stood there looking at us. She was wearing a denim skirt that hung almost to her ankles and a white blouse with a Peter Pan collar.

"Hi, Lonnette," I said. "Remember me?"

"Yes, you're the sheriff," she answered, standing in the doorway looking down at us.

"Mind if we come in?"

She shook her head. "Not supposed to let people in the trailer when Mama's not here."

I looked around. There was a broken-down picnic table between their trailer and the one next to it. Pointing at it, I said, "You wanna come out here and sit?"

"That ain't our table," Lonnette said.

I took her arm and gently pulled her down the steps of the trailer house. "This being police business, I'm sure the owners won't mind, Lonnette."

"Okay," she said, following us.

She sat at the table in almost the exact same pose her mother had taken at the table at the school—feet crossed under her, hands clasped in front of her. I introduced her to Bill.

"Miss Moon," Bill started.

"Lonnette," Lonnette said. "Miz Moon's my mama."

"Okay, Lonnette, you mind if I ask you a few questions?"

"No," she said.

"When was the last time you saw your daddy?"

"I don't know," she said, shrugging.

"Did you see him when he came by to see Tula?" I asked her.

"He came by to see Tula a lot," Lonnette said. "I seen him some when he come by."

"What about the night before he was kilt, Lonnette?" Bill asked. "Did you see him then?"

"Sir?" she asked.

I held up my hand to Bill. "Lonnette," I said gently. "What day's today?"

She frowned at me. "Friday?"

"And what day's tomorrow?" I asked.

"Tuesday?" she answered. When I didn't respond, she said, "January?"

I smiled and patted her hand. "Thank you, Lonnette, for talking to me and Deputy Williams here. You been a real good girl."

She smiled. "Daddy always said I was a good girl."

"And he was right," I said, standing.

Lonnette walked with us back to the door of the trailer, where our two cars were parked only steps away. An old rattletrap Chevy pickup pulled up and parked next to my squad car and Edna Earle climbed out of the cab.

"Sheriff," she said, nodding her head at me.

"Hey, Miz Moon," I said, turning red as a schoolboy caught peeking in the girls' locker room. "We just wanted to speak with Lonnette a minute."

"You done?" she asked.

"Yes, ma'am," Bill and I answered in unison.

To Lonnette, Edna Earle said, "Get back in the house, Lonnette."

"I done okay, Mama," Lonnette said.

"That's good, honey," Edna Earle said, smiling for the first time in my memory. "You go on in and see about a snack for Tula. She be home in a little while."

"Okay, Mama," Lonnette said and went inside the trailer, shutting the door after her.

"Ever again you wanna see my girls, Sheriff, I'd look kindly on it if you was to ask me first," Edna Earle said, her voice soft and quiet.

"Yes, ma'am," I said, looking at my feet.

She turned and went up the steps of the trailer, opening the door and shutting it gently behind her.

Bill and I didn't exchange a word, just got in our respective squad cars and drove away, both awash in our thoughts of lost little girls and protective mamas.

On the way back to Longbranch, I ruminated some on who shot Dalton and why. It had been only two weeks since somebody had wired my '55 to blow me to hell and back. And now somebody takes a shot at the parking lot of the sheriff's department with me standing there. I couldn't help but think that the bullet that felled Dalton had been meant for me.

Why? Now, normally, murderers don't mess around with lots of different things. They find one thing that works, they stick with it. Wade Moon had been hit over the head with an oar and drowned. Course, I hadn't been near the water in a while and it would be kinda hard for his murderer to fell me with an oar and drown me when the nearest I got to water was my bathtub. It would mean changing their MO just a bit. And the bomb in the car hadn't worked, so they took to shooting at me. Now, of course, that hadn't worked either.

My hands shook a little on the steering wheel of the car. Somebody was trying to kill me. They almost got my nephew

Leonard, and now Dalton Pettigrew, big, dumb, gentle Dalton lay in a hospital bed with his shoulder shot to shit. Jean could be the next miss. Or Melissa or Rebecca or my sister Jewel or anybody fool enough to get near me.

But I wasn't doing shit as far as the Wade Moon case went. I had absolutely no leads and nowhere to go and, goddammit, it wasn't even my case! Why not shoot at Bill Williams?

Okay. It had to do with the animal mutilations. But I was no further along with those than Bill was with the Wade Moon thing. I had absolutely no idea what was going on or why. Which meant only one thing: Emmett Hopkins had been right. They weren't trying to get me personally out of the way. They just decided that I was going to be their first human sacrifice. They were tired of dogs and cats and I was the next step up the food chain, as Emmett had said. Which meant I had to find me some Satanists and I had to find them damn quick.

◀ 15 ▶

I headed back to the station, stopping at a Kwik Stop for a pack of cigarettes. I wanted a smoke bad. Having people shoot at me seemed to do that to me. I bought the pack and walked with it back to the squad car. There was a trash can between me and the car. I lifted the pack to my nose, took a deep sniff, and tossed it in the trash. Expensive habit, but it seemed to help.

I got back to the station around three and went straight to the storage room. In there, gathering dust for the past couple of years, was a whole box of armored vests. The highest tech available at the convention in Dallas that the sheriff went to back in '85. There were five of 'em. Dark blue nylon over something magic that stopped everything but a Teflon bullet. I got 'em out, dusted 'em off, and took 'em into the big room where everybody, including my night deputies, still stood around jawing about Dalton's being shot.

I handed out the vests, one for each of us, including Gladys. "Wear 'em," I said. "Now! Put 'em on. We don't know what the shit's going on here. Whoever it was could stroll right through that front door with a .357 for all we know."

"These are hot, Milt," Jasmine whined.

"Hell of a lot cooler than a slug in the shoulder, Jasmine," I said. " 'Sides, it's winter. We don't catch this sucker by spring, then we'll worry about hot."

Gladys was the first to put hers on, her eyes darting to the front door, no doubt imagining hordes of marauders barging in. After she got the vest on and fastened, she handed me my messages.

Millard Running Deer had called twice to see if we'd had any news on his animals; my wife called to say she'd be late getting home to dinner and don't try to call back because she'd be in meetings with the hospital administrator most of the afternoon; and Melissa had called. Could I call back?

I did.

"Robinson," she said on picking up the phone.

"Hey, Robinson," I said, using a deep, gruff voice, "this is Kovak."

"Hi, look, we've got it all planned! This Saturday. I'm handling the refreshments, Martha's handling the decorations, and Lisa's handling—"

"What are you talking about?" I cut in.

"The party! For the girls? The 'it's okay you didn't get invited to Mindy's birthday party because you're ethnic' party. Remember?"

"Oh. Right. So, what do I need to do?" I asked.

"Call Uncle Rufe. Make sure this Saturday's okay. We'll need an indoor spot for the food and party and then the horses if the weather's okay."

"The only reason we're doing this at Uncle Rufe's is 'cause of the horses, Melissa—"

"The weatherman's talking snow."

"So? They can't ride horseback in the snow? Give 'em a nice soft landing when they fall on their little butts."

"I thought you said these horses of his were gentle?" she demanded.

"It was a joke."

"Don't joke with a mother about her kid falling off a horse, Milt. It's not funny." She sighed. "Now, speaking of funny—what have you done to the Reynolds family that you shouldn't have done?"

I grinned. "Oh, a little of this and a little of that."

"Opal Allen says they're thinking of taking Mindy out of her day care."

"You're kidding! Because of me?"

"Well, I don't know, Milt. Maybe if you'd tell me what you've done?"

I felt bad about that. I hadn't thought of the consequences of my actions. That they might hurt the little girl Mindy. Of all of them, she was the only innocent one. I sighed. "I've just harassed them some, that's all."

"Like what?" Melissa insisted.

"Well, I don't know! Just a little . . . you know . . . harassment. Legal harassment. Checking to make sure they're up to city and county codes."

"Milton, I swear to God!" she said, sounding a whole hell of a lot like her mama.

"You knew I was gonna do it!" I said, shifting a little accessory-before-and-after-the-fact blame where it squarely belonged.

"Well, stop!" Melissa said.

"Okay," I answered, realizing I was definitely pouting. The next thing on my agenda had been a doozy. It had initials that spelled IRS.

I got off the phone and sat around thinking for a while. Thinking maybe my retribution had gone a bit too far, thinking about Wade Moon rising out of the water, thinking about mutilated puppy dogs and kitty cats, thinking about the shell of my '55 and Dalton's messed-up shoulder, thinking about wives and sisters and a little boy who was going to wonder why his daddy didn't have the breath to play ball in the front yard or the strength to handle the father-and-son football game at the high school. In other words, I sat around for about forty minutes and wallowed in self-righteous self-pity.

A little after four, Gladys called on the intercom to say I had a phone call from Jared Blessing.

"I'll take it," I said, hitting the blinking button on the telephone. "Jared?" I said.

"Sheriff?" he whispered.

"Yeah, Jared, I can barely hear you."

"I gotta whisper! I don't know who might be listening!"

"Okay. What's up?" I asked.

"I got myself invited to a party—"

"A what?"

"A party! With some headbangers!"

"Some what?"

"Headbangers!" he said loudly.

I held the phone away from my ear, then put it back. "Okay, boy, I give up. What the hell's a headbanger?"

"You know, a waver! Headbanger!"

"Uh-huh," I said.

I heard his sigh of exasperation. "They're the ones who probably did it, Sheriff!"

"Did what?" The boy had totally lost me now.

"The animals!"

"Oh! You're going to one of their parties?"

"Yeah," he whispered, "Friday night! I wangled an invite through Lyla Miller."

"Miller?"

"The girl I was telling you about with the three earrings in each ear!"

"Oh, right. She's a banger?"

"Headbanger or waver. That means new wave. Ya know?"

No, I didn't know, but I wasn't gonna let this punk kid think I couldn't keep up on what's current. I'd ask my nephew. Not that he'd tell me the truth.

"So," I said, "a party. What kind of party?"

"That's just it, Sheriff," he whispered, "I think this might be where they do it! You want me to wear a wire?"

Oh, shit, I thought. The boy's been watching "Starsky and Hutch" reruns again. "Well, Jared, that would be real handy, if we had anything like that here but we don't. Why don't you just call me if anything comes up?"

"Roger," he said, I swear to God. "I'll keep you posted." And he hung up without even saying goodbye, but I guess James Bond never was big on the niceties either.

As I was getting my things together to take my leave for the hospital, Bill Williams called from Tejas County. The long-distance bills were gonna get ridiculous if we didn't find out who killed Wade Moon pretty damn quick.

"You set up another interview?" he asked.

"With who?" I asked.

"Anybody, boy. I ain't proud!"

"Well, you were talking about Bernice Strom earlier," I reminded.

"Yeah, that'd be good. Or the widow. Or both."

"Okay, I'll set it up for tomorrow," I said. Then thinking how this was really his case and his county should have to handle the long-distance bills, not mine, I said, "Call me tomorrow morning and I'll let you know when."

"Will do," he said and hung up, leaving me with the feeling that I was the only person who didn't have a "Dragnet" complex.

So I made the phone calls, catching Gayla at her mama's house and making an appointment to talk to them both at the Strom home right outside Longbranch the next day around eleven A.M.

I got to the hospital around five. I stopped by my wife's office but she wasn't in and Bette Raintree had apparently already left for the day. Melissa was in her office but when I started to stick my head in her door, I heard a voice I didn't want to hear. Namely, my deputy Mike Neils. Him and Melissa were giggling fit to beat the band and, personally, that was something I didn't want to hear. I went on down a floor to Dalton's room.

Dalton lay asleep in his bed, his mama sitting in a chair next to him, her Bible in her lap. She looked up when I came in and put a finger to her lips. I motioned her outside where we stood in the hall to talk.

"How's he doing, Miz Pettigrew?" I asked.

"Tolerable," she said. "They got him on some sleepy medzine. Cain't hardly keep his eyes open."

"Well, that's probably for the best," I said. "Miz Pettigrew, I want to apologize about Dalton getting hurt. I think that bullet was probably meant for me, ma'am, and, well . . ."

Dalton's mother shook her head. "That boy woulda dried up and blowed away if he couldn'ta been a sheriff's deputy. All he ever talked about since the time he could walk straight." She shook her head again. "I always knowed something like this was gonna happen, and if he heals up proper, I know he's gonna go back to it. I just give it all to Jesus, Sheriff. Onliest thing I can do."

I smiled and patted her thin shoulder. "Yes, ma'am," I said. "I guess you're right. Tell Dalton I came by and I'll be back in the morning."

Then I went home to heat myself some Lean Quizine.

The Strom home had once been Judge Lloyd Cooley's home, which had originally belonged to his wife's daddy, Marshant Stewart Rice, one of the richest men to ever come out of

Prophesy County, Oklahoma. The house had been built long before statehood and had been added on to as the money grew in the family. It sorta looked like Tara with wings.

It had grounds and outbuildings, columns, gables, and twelve outside doors. I always figured you could tell the wealth of a man by how many outside doors his house had. My brother-in-law had six, not counting the garage, but, then again, I got four, so I ain't doing so poorly my ownself.

Bill had met me at the sheriff's department and we'd driven to the house on the outskirts of town together, pulling into the circular driveway in my squad car and parking right by the front door. Which was a good thing since a cold snap had hit in the middle of the night, bringing the temperature down to twenty with a windchill factor of minus ten, and a wind out of the north blowing about twenty miles a hour. The bridges were iced over and county crews had been out since before dawn sanding as many as they could. But as the locals say, it was just too damn cold to snow.

We rang the bell and a black woman in a black dress with a starched white apron opened the door almost immediately. She was my first outside the movies—uniformed hired help. I was impressed in spite of myself.

Bill and I introduced ourselves and she ushered us into the foyer without saying a word, then she moved off, leaving us standing there. Halfway across the foyer, she looked back and said, "You coming?"

"Yes, ma'am," Bill and I said in unison and followed at a smart pace.

Besides the hotel me and Jean stayed at in Mexico, this was the fanciest place I'd ever seen. The foyer, tiled in black and white, just like in the movies, was two stories high and had a graceful, wide staircase leading up to a wide landing. Two other staircases went in opposite directions from the landing to the second floor. There was nothing much in the foyer 'cept some throw rugs and pictures.

We followed the maid down a short hall to an opening that led to what appeared to be a breakfast room. It was too small to be this house's main dining room, as there was only a small round table with seating for four, an antique dry sink, and, down two steps, an area with rattan sofas and chairs with big windows looking out at the winter-blown garden beyond. Looking at all that, I figured I could live this way without too much adjustment.

Bernice Strom and Gayla Moon were sitting in green floral-print rattan chairs down the two steps. Bill and I circled the table and went down the steps to meet them.

I held out my hand to both and so did Bill.

"Please, Sheriff, Deputy, won't you have a seat?" Mrs. Strom said.

I looked at her. I'd never seen Bernice Strom before. All my dealings had been with her husband. And I knew that Ulysses wasn't where Gayla had got her looks. They clearly came from her mother. She had to be at least my age, early to midfifties, but she was one of the prettiest women I'd ever seen. I figured all those people who thought Ulysses married her for her money were blind or stupid.

Like her daughter, she had red hair, now fading slightly, not as bright as her daughter's. A blond streak that coulda been gray ran from just above her temple to the back of her hair, which was cut medium length and worn kinda puffy, like women wear it on TV. Her hand, when she had given it to me, was small and barely marked with age, but then again, she did have a maid. The nails were painted a frosted dark pink shade that matched her lipstick. The skin on her face was as perfect as her daughter's, with the tiny blue veins peeking through from underneath. Around her cobalt blue eyes were just faint wrinkles almost totally hidden by some kind of magic with makeup.

She was wearing a blue raw silk tunic (I only know it was raw silk because Jean bought a top to go to Mexico that was raw silk, and if God ever made anything classier-looking, he's keeping it to himself) with white pants, a strand of pearls at her neck. The lady was definitely more Park Avenue than Prophesy County, Oklahoma, but then, class ain't got no geography.

Gayla was as coiffed and manicured as her mama, but her eyes had dark circles and her skin had lost some of its sheen.

"I'm sorry to be bothering you two lovely ladies like this," I said, smiling. They returned my smile. "But we're running into a dead end on this thing with Wade. We need to ask you both some questions, if you don't mind."

Mrs. Strom smiled. "We don't mind at all, Sheriff. But you must understand my husband is an attorney, and well, you know how they are!" She laughed lightly. Her voice dripped with honey and her laugh was like the tinkle of fairy bells. If I wasn't a married man, I'da fallen at her feet with words of undying love. Or at least thought about it.

"Ma'am?" was all I could manage.

"Daddy said not to answer any of your questions until he gets here, Milt," Gayla said. She shrugged and smiled. "Lawyers."

We all laughed politely, me and Bill and Mrs. Strom and Gayla.

"Would you gentlemen like some coffee?" Mrs. Strom asked. "Merline makes the best Louisiana coffee you ever had in your whole life." Turning from us she rang the bell sitting beside her on a rattan table. "Merline, honey," she said when the maid appeared. "Some of your wonderful coffee and . . . oh! Some of those delicious popovers! You still have some left?"

"Yes, ma'am," Merline said, turning and walking away.

Mrs. Strom turned back to Bill and me and smiled. "Looks like we're finally going to get some real winter," she said.

"Yes, ma'am," I answered. "They're talking about snow."

Mrs. Strom shook her beautiful head. "Too cold to snow. Though we'll be seeing plenty of ice."

"That'll certainly keep Milt and me busy," Bill said, smiling and staring at Mrs. Strom fit to beat the band. "Car wrecks and such," he said by way of explanation. An unnecessary one to my way of thinking.

"You both have such incredibly responsible jobs," Mrs. Strom said, her face serious. "But all the horrors you see must take their toll!"

Bill leaned forward on the rattan sofa, his face serious to match hers, a look of incredibly responsible concern on his face. "You learn to live with the grief, Mrs. Strom. But, believe me, sometimes, it gets me, right here." And he pointed at his heart.

Mrs. Strom leaned forward and patted his hand where it rested on his knee. "How could it not?" she said, then smiled. "You're only human."

I was hoping Ulysses Strom would get there quick before I broke my lifetime record and puked.

Merline arrived with the coffee and popovers on a silver tray. The coffee was in a silver urn and the popovers sat on individual silver and glass plates. Merline sat the tray down on the rattan coffee table and left, not saying a word.

Mrs. Strom loosened the vacuum top of the coffee urn and lifted it, pouring dark, rich-smelling coffee into cups. "Cream?" she said smiling. "Sugar or sweetener?"

We fixed our coffee and Bill and I both took plates with popovers. Mrs. Strom handed us each a linen napkin. I felt like if I spoke at that moment, my words would come out with a British accent.

At a sound in the hallway, Gayla jumped up. "That must be Daddy!" she said, heading up the two steps into the breakfast room. Ulysses Strom came in the door of the room and kissed his daughter on the cheek, then, with his arm around her waist, walked her back down the steps. Bill and I set down our goodies and stood as Ulysses leaned down and pecked his wife on the cheek. Standing, he shook both our hands.

"Well, boys," he said, pulling one of the table chairs down to the lower level and straddling it, taking a popover off a plate and nibbling at it, crumbs dropping on the Oriental rug covering the floor, "I was hoping our little talk the other day woulda been enough that you wouldn't need to go bothering my womenfolk."

"Well, Mr. Strom," I said smiling, "I'm sorry, but we've got to question everybody who knew Wade. It's just procedure."

He waved his hand at me in dismissal. "Go ahead and ask your questions, but if you ask something I don't like, I'm gonna tell my girls not to answer you. Got that?"

"Yes, sir," Bill and I both said.

I turned to Gayla. "Gayla, I'm sorry to have to bring all this up again, but can you tell me what time Wade left that morning?"

Gayla shook her pretty head. "Not really, Milt. I would say it was around five-thirty or six, that's when he usually left for Lake Blue. He went every morning, you know."

"That's what I understood," I said, nodding. "Were you awake when he left?"

Gayla laughed, a tinkly little laugh, not unlike her mother's. "Lord no!" she said. "Wade was the early riser, not me! I usually don't get up until eight-thirty or nine."

Bill spoke up. "Was there anything on Wade's mind that you noticed?"

Gayla cocked her head. "Pardon?"

"Like was he worried about something? Scared of somebody? Anything like that?" Bill asked.

Gayla shook her head. "No. He seemed fine. Excited about running for sheriff."

Low blow, I thought to myself, wondering what Bill had going in his mind at the mention of the sheriff's race.

Bill lowered his head, sighed, then looked up again. "Miz Moon, I hate to bring this up, but I gotta. It's come to my attention that though Wade led everybody to believe he was a sergeant with the OHP, that the truth was he was a civilian file clerk."

Gayla glanced at her father, who nodded. Turning back to Bill and me, she said, "Wade was a very proud man, Deputy Williams." She sighed. "When we ran away the way we did, he gave up a job that meant everything to him. He wanted very much to go back to work in law enforcement. But Wade got on with the Prophesy sheriff's office before deputies had to go through the academy like they do now"—which is exactly how me and Bill both got on at our respective jobs—"and he tried, I mean, he really tried to get through the academy. But he just couldn't do the academics. I tried to help, but I could only do so much. He took the job as a file clerk after flunking out of the academy, thinking he'd work there for a while, study, and then try again." She shrugged. "He just never got around to it."

"Wade was only with the OHP for twelve years," I said. "How'd he come to retire like that? I mean, even a civilian has to put in at least twenty or reach sixty-five, right?"

Ulysses Strom stood up. "Sheriff, my wife's got a hair appointment in town and my daughter's on her way to do some shopping. I think they've answered enough questions."

Well, I begged to differ, since Gayla hadn't answered the one I'd just asked and we hadn't even got to Mrs. Strom yet. But laywers are lawyers and rich lawyers are something else again. And politics being politics, Bill and I took our leave.

◀ 16 ▶

The circular drive in front of the house was beginning to resemble a used car lot when me and Bill got into my squad car to head out. We had to pull around what I presumed to be Gayla's car—a brand-new BMW, probably a sorry-you-got-widowed gift from her daddy. Blocking us from the back were a beat-up old Chevy pickup and Ulysses Strom's white-on-white Cadillac.

We pulled our car coat collars up around our ears as we got in the squad car, me turning the heat up to high, even though it didn't even start to affect the cold until we were halfway to Longbranch. The extra bulk of the armored vest kept me some warm and I worried just a bit about Bill not having one on. But we only had the five.

Back at the station house, Bill got into his car and headed back to Tejas County, none the wiser for the morning's work, of course, and I headed on into my office. The freeze had caused a rash of accidents on the county roads and highways, most of 'em fender benders, with the exception of one that Mike Neils was out on when I came in. I asked Gladys about it.

"Three-car collision," she said, writing in her log while she spoke. "Don't know who yet. Told Mike to call in as soon as he could. Don't know if there are any fatalities either, but an ambulance got sent just the same."

I walked toward my office. "Keep me posted," I said over my shoulder.

Two hours later, Mike came into my office. "Sit," I said. He sat. I leaned back in my chair, my feet on my desk, and waited.

"Old man Newsome pulled out of his driveway and ran smack dab into some siding salesman from Oklahoma City. Then Miz Bittehurtz ran into the back of the salesman and her kid wasn't in a seat belt and he fell to the floor in the front seat, knotting his head." He sighed. "It was a godawful mess, Milt, I want you to know."

"How's the siding salesman?"

"Meaner than piss." He shook his head. "Got a broken arm when Mr. Newsome backed into the driver's door and looks like whiplash when Miz Bittehurtz slammed into the back of him. Then Ricky Martin, he was on the stretcher, slammed the door of the ambulance and caught the guy's foot. Guy ain't had a great day." Mike grinned and I started to laugh. "Milt, you could hear that guy screaming for a country mile! 'I'm suing!' "

"Who's he gonna sue?" I asked, grinning.

Mike shrugged. "Everybody."

"How's Miz Bittehurtz's kid?"

"A good-sized bump. Doctor told her to watch him for concussion and she took him on home."

"Well, no fatalities, that's good."

Mike headed on out the door and I called Uncle Rufe to make plans about Saturday. He was happy as a pup with an extra tit, as he said, and I wondered about the brilliance of me even showing up at the party. I could be putting my kith and kin, not to mention some innocent little girls, in jeopardy.

By Tuesday the temperature had risen to thirty degrees but the overcast skies remained. That afternoon, it started to snow. I got fourteen calls from Melissa and the other mothers wondering whether we should have this party or not, and I just kept telling them to make their decisions their ownselves and leave me out of it. Wednesday morning I woke up to five inches of snow and a telephone call from A.B. Tate, on night duty at the station, telling me we had people stuck in the snow in three places he was aware of around the county, one missing child, and a rash of auto accidents.

By Wednesday afternoon we'd found the three people reported stuck in their cars in the snow drifts from the morning, had four more, found the kid building a snowman out behind the garage, and had taken two people to the hospital with minor cuts and bruises from the morning auto accidents and were en route with the afternoon auto accident victims. Me? I just love snow. 'Bout as much as a hot fudge enema.

Thursday the sun came out, the temperature rose to forty-five degrees, the streets were clear, and we were almost back to normal. Except that a pile of snow next to the Tastee-Freez's back door melted, ran in under the door without anybody seeing it, touched on a frayed cord on the floor, knocked out the wiring, and caused both the fire alarm and the burglar alarm to go off simultaneously.

Glenn Jackson who owns the Tastee-Freez tried to hold back the panic, but Julie Marie Mason and Dusty Rose Mahoney (her mama's got four girls—all named after fingernail polish), the two girls behind the counter at the Tastee-Freez, started a rush out the front door screaming their lungs out and the three patrons followed suit, knocking over tables with hot chocolate, ice cream treats and other confections to the floor, making such a mess that Glenn Jackson, in his attempt to stop the panic, fell in spilled ice cream and broke his hip. Which just goes to show you that snow, in any form, never did nobody any good.

Friday morning Millard Running Deer called to say two more

cats had been found mutilated and left in the middle of the road in front of the shelter. The night guard saw a car pulling away but didn't get a make or license. His only information was that its color was dark. I went on over and got the poor animals and took 'em to Dr. Jim, who wasn't all that thrilled about it.

Friday night around eleven o'clock, while I lay in bed admiring the beginning of a little bulge in my wife's lovely stomach, the phone rang. I picked it up, because, being sheriff, it's expected of me.

"Kovak," I said.

"Hey, Milt, it's Emmett."

"Hey, yourself."

"How's that new Jeep?"

"Just great. What's up?"

"Well, I got me a young man in custody here claims he works for you."

"No shit? Who is he and why's he in custody?" I asked.

"Well, now, he won't give out his name and he don't have any ID on him neither. He's in custody for driving under the influence and generally being a nuisance."

"Well, maybe you could put this mystery man on the phone."

"Maybe I could do that," Emmett said.

In a moment, another voice, a whispered voice, said, "Sheriff?"

"Now who am I speaking to?" I asked.

"Sheriff! It's me!" he whispered urgently. "Your undercover man at the you-know-where."

I've been known to be slow, a little lazy maybe, quarrelsome, lots of other things, but never particularly stupid. I said, "Jared, you're in deep shit, little buddy."

"No, no!" he whispered. "Listen, Sheriff! They made me drink! I had to if I was going to find out anything for you! Don't you see?"

"Jared—"

"Listen! Listen! Don't let the chief call my daddy, hear? He can't call my daddy, Sheriff! You understand?"

"Jared, you are drunk on your butt."

"No, sir, no, sir. Just a little. Just a little drunk on my butt. Not *real* drunk on my butt, you understand?"

"Well, did you at least find anything out for me, boy?"

"Whooee, yes, sir! Whooee!"

I held the phone away from my ear. Replacing it, I said, "What?"

"They drink, Sheriff!"

I put my hand over the mouthpiece to keep from laughing out loud. Finally, I said, "Well, we'll have to do something about that—"

"And Sheriff—"

"Yes, Jared?"

He belched in my ear. " 'Cuse me, Sheriff."

"It's okay, Jared."

"Sheriff—"

"Yes, Jared?"

"They fornicate."

"Do they now?" I said.

"Yes, sir. These two couples went in another room and I thought that was probably where they kept the . . . you, know . . . the—"

"Booze?"

"No . . ."

"Dope?"

"No . . ."

"What, Jared?"

He sighed. In a confused voice, he said, "Sheriff, why was I doing this?"

"The animals?" I ventured.

"Whooee! That's right!" He laughed. "Lord almighty, I almost forgot! That's why I followed them because I thought that's where they were doing those devil things with the animals . . . but, Sheriff . . ."

"Yes, Jared?"

"They were fornicating."

"Well, Jared, I'm sorry you had to see that."

"But, Sheriff, I been thinking . . ."

"Yes, Jared?"

"You think Lyla Miller'd let me—"

"Jared, let me speak to the police chief."

When Emmett got back on the line, I said, "Look, the boy was sorta working for me. In a half-assed sorta way. Though I had nothing to do with him getting drunk—"

"You ever gonna tell me the story behind this, Milt?" Emmett asked.

"One of these days. Meanwhile, any way you can sober him up and get him home without his daddy knowing about this? His daddy's Gary Blessing, music director over at the First Baptist."

"Whoa, shit." He was silent for a moment and I let him be. Then he said, "Okay. I'll do what I can. But if this comes out, Milt, it's your ass."

"And a fine one it is, too," I said and hung up.

Saturday morning dawned fresh as a spring breeze. The temperature was in the upper fifties, the sky was a cobalt blue with little white puffy clouds, and there was a light southerly breeze. The ground was a little wet from melted snow and some of the white stuff could still be seen by fence posts and in ditches, but it was a picture-perfect day. Jean rearranged her schedule and came with me to Uncle Rufe's for the party.

The horses were three gentle mares and, after the initial fear of getting on such big creatures, the girls had a great time. We were in the middle of ice cream and cake when my beeper went off. I excused myself and went into Uncle Rufe's den to call the station.

Jasmine Bodine answered my call. "Hey, Milt," she said, despondently, but then again, Jasmine says everything despondently. It's her nature.

"Hey, Jasmine. What's up?"

"Well, I picked up Dalton this morning and took him home," she said.

"That's great," I said, "How's he doing?"

"Okay, I guess." Jasmine sounded on the verge of tears, but then again, she always did. "Oh, and Chief Hopkins called you just now. Said for you to call him back right away."

"Thanks, Jasmine," I said, hanging up and dialing the police department's number.

When I got through to Emmett, he said, "Milt, got something for you. Got a call a little while ago about some animals letting out a bunch of noise at a house over on Kennard."

"No shit?"

"I'm on my way. You wanna meet me?"

He didn't have to ask me twice. I kissed all the appropriate people at the party goodbye and got in my new Jeep, heading for town.

Kennard Street is two blocks from the downtown area of Longbranch but runs almost to the city limits, about three miles long. The address Emmett had given me on Kennard was a one-story clapboard house on about an acre of land. I pulled up behind Emmett's squad car. Behind me, I could hear an ambulance siren screaming down the street.

I got out of the car and went up to the front door, which stood open, the glass-and-aluminum storm door the only thing between me and the scene inside the living room of the clapboard house. I opened the storm door and walked in.

Emmett stood in front of an old man, about seventy, who sat on an orange vinyl couch, his head in his hands. In front of him, newspapers spread on the coffee table between him and Emmett, lay a dead dog.

Emmett turned when he heard me. Bending down, he picked up some other newspapers and spread them over the dead animal.

"Milton," he said.

"Emmett," I said. "What we got here?"

Pointing at the old man, Emmett said, "This is Taylor Albright. Mr. Albright, this is the county sheriff, Milton Kovak."

The old man looked up, his eyes puffy and red, his wrinkled skin sallow and drawn. "Sheriff," he said, his thin voice barely audible.

"The animal shelter is in Sheriff Kovak's jurisdiction, Mr. Albright. So the sheriff's probably gonna want to ask you some questions."

I looked at the old man again. He looked familiar. "Mr. Albright," I said, "don't you attend the First Baptist?"

He looked up. "Yes, sir. I do. My wife's a member of the choir."

The ambulance stopped outside the Albright house. I thought it a little strange for Emmett to be calling an ambulance for a dead dog, but then again, I didn't say anything.

"At least she was," Mr. Albright said, and started crying.

Emmett moved away from Mr. Albright to a doorway that led into a hall. "Mrs. Emmy Albright's right in here, Milt."

I looked in the door of the first bedroom. Mrs. Albright lay under the covers of the bed, her hands folded on her stomach, a bouquet of flowers in her hands. Obviously pretty much dead.

Pill bottles adorned the little nightstand next to the bed. Emmett and I walked back into the living room to let in the ambulance attendants.

I went and sat down next to Mr. Albright on the sofa. I patted his hand. "What happened, Mr. Albright?" I asked.

"The cancer," he said, his voice a whisper. "We tried everything. We tried the chemo, radiation, we tried giving it to Jesus. We took all our life savings last year and went down to Mexico for this treatment they got down there." He sighed. "Didn't do no good."

I shook my head. "I'm real sorry, Mr. Albright. But, I just don't understand about the animals."

"Emmy's from Louisiana originally, though she's been here in Oklahoma since 1948, when I brought her here after the war. I was stationed in New Orleans for a while in '45. That's when I met her and we got married. When I mustered out in '48, we come on back here to live with my kin."

"Yes, sir," I said, nodding, not knowing where this was leading.

"The Lord never blessed us with any children, Sheriff. It was always just me and Emmy. We took care of some nieces and nephews for a spell when my brother and his wife split up, but that was just for a year or two. And we had a grandniece living with us for a spell back in '74. But no children of our own."

"I'm sorry for that, Mr. Albright," I said, biding my time.

"Emmy's real name was Emualine, Sheriff. She was Cajun. Her mama was a witch, they say. Miss Antoinette, that's Emmy's mama, she believed in what they call the 'gri-gri.' You ever hear tell of that, Sheriff?"

"Not that I know of," I answered truthfully.

"That's some kind of spell and witchcraft kinda stuff. Not that

I'd want anybody at the First Baptist knowing about this, Sheriff," he said.

I nodded my head, even though I knew this would be all over town in a New York minute. Even boring stuff gets around that fast.

"Well, when the doctor told us Emmy was in the final stages of the cancer, that she was gonna die in less than six months, she said maybe we could do some gri-gri. I woulda done anything, Sheriff, anything to save my Emmy."

He broke down and started bawling. I put my arm around the old man's thin shoulders and held him while he cried.

After a while, he sighed and looked up at me. " 'Twere supposed to be chickens but the only person around here got chickens is Tom Evans over towards the highway. I tried to get in and get me some, but he's got this real tall fence and I'm just too blamed old to climb it." He sighed. "But then Emmy said dogs or cats would work too, so that's why we went to the animal shelter. The cats were pretty awful," he said. "But I never did much like cats. But I sure hated hurting them dogs."

I stood up from the couch and moved around the coffee table, the dead dog between us.

"Mr. Albright, I don't think I understand about this gri-gri business. You wanna explain?"

The old man sighed. "Oh, hell, Sheriff, I don't know much about it myself. I just got the animals like my Emmy tole me and I brung 'em home. Then she'd say some Cajun words over 'em and tell me what to do."

"And that was?"

Mr. Albright looked up at me, his eyes brimming with tears. "Son, you don't really wanna know that."

I sighed. "Okay, did you do 'em one at a time or what? And

why dispose of them the way you did? If you'da buried them, nobody woulda known what was going on."

"We did one animal a night. Sometimes I'd hold on to 'em and dispose of 'em a few at a time. The gri-gri Emmy's mama taught her says the devil's gotta see what you done. Emmy said if we buried 'em, the devil wouldn't know. We had to leave 'em out in the open for him to see."

"Mr. Albright," I said, "you mind me saying that's the dumbest fool thing I ever heard of?"

The old man shook his head. "I can't say I disagree with you, Sheriff," he said. "Me being a good Baptist and all. But . . ." He choked back a sob. "I'da poked myself blind if it'da meant another year with my Emmy."

"Mr. Albright," I said, "why did you put a bomb in my car and try to shoot at me?"

He looked up with his red-rimmed eyes. "Pardon?"

I repeated my question.

"You in the car when it went up, Sheriff?"

I explained about the bomb, the puff of smoke and escaping the car at the last minute.

He lifted his shoulders proudly. "Sheriff, I was a demolitions expert in the army. If I'da wanted to blow you up, boy, you'd be in little pieces right now."

"You didn't try to shoot me either, huh?" I asked.

He shook his head. "No, sir, I surely didn't."

We took Mr. Albright into the station, while I wondered just who the hell it was who was trying to kill my frail pink ass.

◀ 17 ▶

Once at the station, I handed Mr. Albright over to Jasmine and called Uncle Rufe's place to see if Millard Running Deer was still there. He was just on his way out the door, but I managed to catch him.

"It's over, Millard," I said. "There's one cat and one dog left. Meet me at the station and I'll take you to where they are."

"Who the hell was it?" Millard demanded.

"I'll explain it all when you get here," I said and hung up.

The last two animals had been in a pen in the backyard. They were cold and wet and hungry, and Emmett and I had taken them out of the pen and put them in the garage with some food from the refrigerator and some milk and water. That's all we could think of. The rest would be up to Millard.

I got back to the house around five that evening. Jean had been driven home by Melissa and the two women and Rebecca were sitting in the living room replaying the day when I walked in.

Rebecca ran to me and threw her arms around my leg as I came in the door. "Oh, Grandpa! I loved it! I want my own horse! Please! Please!"

"Honey, I bet Uncle Rufe would let you come by and ride that horse anytime you want," I said, picking her up and carrying her into the living room.

"Yeah, but I want Buttercup to live with me! In my room!"

"Oh, now, a horse is too big to live in a house, honey."

"Buttercup's not. She's just the right size, right, Mommy?"

I heard a noise and looked over at the foyer. Evinrude sat with his back to me, staring at the foyer wall. His tail lay straight out on the floor. I walked up to him, leaned down and petted his head. He didn't move a muscle.

"It's all over, boy," I told him. "You can go out now."

Still he didn't move. I walked to the front door and opened it. He stood, walked stiffly past me, not even glancing in my direction, and walked sedately out onto the front porch, where he stood for a moment, surveying his domain. Then, with one quick, backward glance, he bounded off the steps and off into the darkening night. I figured it was probably time to get him fixed, but then, that was something me and him would just have to think about.

I walked back into the living room. "You found whoever stole the animals at the shelter," Jean said, smiling.

"Yeah, I'll give you the details later," I said, not wanting to talk about it in front of Rebecca.

"Well," Melissa said, rising and taking Rebecca by the hand, "it's been a long day." She kissed Jean and then me on the cheek, as did Rebecca, and I walked them to the door.

I went back into the living room and sat down on the sofa next to my wife, and told her the sad tale of Taylor and Emmy Albright.

The next two weeks went by, as weeks tend to do. I watched my bride's belly swell up some, which was an awesome sight, and learned what many men tend to learn—that pregnant women are beautiful, when it's your baby in their belly.

We had a leak in the downstairs bathroom and I put on my

plumber's hat (figuratively) and set about fixing it. Two hours later, with half the bathroom destroyed, and at Jean's insistence, I called in a professional.

Things got hopping the way they do over in Tejas County and Bill Williams put the Wade Moon case on a back burner. He called me from time to time, making snide remarks about how'd I like getting away with murder. I laughed at the appropriate places and defended myself at the appropriate places, but it was never serious and the jibing didn't last long.

Jewel and Harmon left in the middle of that time for a week in Hawaii, leaving the kids in the charge of Leonard, the oldest. I went by two or three times during that week, checking to make sure he hadn't killed the younger two and stuffed them in the freezer. Usually, as I suspected, Leonard wasn't even there and Marlene, my niece, had taken over her own care and the care of Carl, the baby. I offered at every visit to have them come and stay with Jean and me, but they were having a good time on their own, so I left it. I figured Leonard was at least there in the wee hours of the night.

The following Sunday, me and Jean had Jewel and Harmon over for dinner to pay them back for the dinner they had us over to. Jean said that's the way it's done. We'd just sat down at the dining room table when Jewel Anne said, "You moved the picture I had on that wall."

"Yes, I did," Jean said tightly.

Jewel looked to the wall where the picture had been moved. She frowned. "I don't know, Jean. I really think it looked better over here. More balance—"

Jean stood up, grabbed her crutches and stuck them under her arms. "Jewel, would you mind stepping into the living room with me?"

Jewel stood uncertainly. "Well, of course not, Jean, but the food—"

"To hell with the food," Jean said, turned and strode across the foyer and into the living room.

Jewel looked at Harmon and me but, being men, we were busily looking at our plates, contemplating the interesting food sitting there. When Jewel left the room, Harmon and I snuck a look at each other, then politely began eating and minding our own business.

We could hear voices coming from the living room, but no words. Finally, we heard Jewel Anne's shoes on the foyer tile, heard the front door open. Jewel said, "Harmon! Now!" and was out the door.

Harmon wiped his mouth, said, "Thanks for the dinner, Milt," shrugged and hightailed it out the door.

I got up from the table and walked into the living room. Jean sat on the sofa, picking at imaginary lint on her black slacks.

"Well?" I said.

She looked up and smiled. "I doubt that it did any good," Jean said, "but I feel a hell of a lot better."

Standing, she came over and kissed me on the lips. "Will it be a problem for you if your sister and I never speak again?"

"I can handle it," I said, stroking her back. "Just don't expect me not to have a relationship with her."

She shook her head. "I don't expect that. I would never expect that."

I grabbed a handful of her butt and suggested we call it a night.

Monday morning, the first week of March, dawned cold and wet. The wet was just a drizzle, but there were evil-looking black clouds to the north. The cold was the raw, wet cold you get in our part of the world. The temperature was only down to fifty, but the cold in your body felt more like minus five.

Driving into Longbranch on Highway 5, I witnessed a car wreck, barely missing involvement myself, and called it in on the cellular phone in my Jeep. (Did I mention I got a cellular phone? They threw it in as an extra. Every Jeep needs a phone. I mean, imagine being out in the middle of the desert, tooling through open country in your Jeep in four-wheel drive, when you get this overpowering urge for a pizza. I mean, think about it.)

One car was a load of kids heading for the high school and another an old farmer in a pickup. He, the farmer, was going too slow, so the girl driving the car tried to pass him on the right. Not that she didn't just learn in driver's ed never to pass on the right, but then again, who ever listens in those classes, right? She hit a patch of mud, spun out, and rolled over, down the ditch, through a barbed-wire fence, and out into an open field. The farmer got panicked, slammed on his brakes, and slid in the sloppy road, turning his car around one hundred and eighty degrees, staring straight at me. I slammed on my brakes, remembering which way to pull the wheel in a skid, and came to a complete stop in my lane of the highway. The two cars behind us got stopped without doing much damage, and, after I called it in, everybody headed down to see about the kids.

And they were scattered all hither and yon. A boy who obviously hadn't been wearing his seat belt lay tangled in the broken barbed wire, blood oozing out of a hundred places on his body. Checking him first, I deemed them mostly superficial cuts from the barbed wire, and went on to a girl lying half in and half out of the car. Her foot was stuck under the front seat and she was pinned pretty good.

The impact of the crash had started the engine to smoking. Bob McCalister who lives down Highway 5 a bit and works in

Longbranch, had been in one of the cars behind me. Him and me tried getting the girl out, but her leg was stuck good.

Three other kids, two more girls and a boy, were out of the car and all in fairly good condition, so we had the tourist couple—a couple in their seventies traveling from Fort Worth to Kansas City to see their kids and show off their new RV, who had been behind Bob when the accident occurred—take the kids to the shelter of the RV and check 'em out. The rain was coming down harder, but not hard enough to stop the engine from bursting into flames.

"Let me get my Jeep!" I yelled at Bob over the downpour.

I ran to the Jeep, started it, put it into four-wheel drive, and headed for the wrecked car. The man from the RV came running out of it carrying a fire extinguisher and used it on the engine of the car. It did some good, but not enough. More of the car was catching on fire, and flames were licking the toes of the girl's Reeboks.

I didn't have time to read the owner's manual. I just grabbed the chain out of the back and hooked it to the winch, ran it over the bottom of the wrecked car (which was now the top) and hooked it to the seat that was holding the girl captive.

"Okay, Bob," I yelled. "I'm gonna start the winch. When you see that sucker move, pull her the hell out!"

Bob gave me a thumbs-up and I ran around the car to the Jeep, hit the thingamabob on the winch, and watched it go to town.

I heard the girl scream, Bob yell, and I ran around the car to see them laying in a heap, free from the wrecked and burning car. Except when I looked back at the wrecked and burning car, it was rolling over from the force of the winch and was being wound up right to my brand-new Jeep.

I yelled "Oh, shit!" and headed for the Jeep, turning off the thingamabob on the winch and unhooking the chain, and backing the Jeep the hell away from the wreck. There is something to be said for reading the instructions immediately upon getting a new playtoy. But then again, I'm a man and not expected to have to play by that rule. As all men know, only women, children, and severely testosterone-impaired men read instructions.

We got everybody in the ambulance when it got there, I left Mike Neils in charge of the cleanup, and I thanked everybody who'd helped. The boy who'd been in the barbed wire had surface cuts and bruises, and the girl who'd got her foot stuck had a burn on her big toe and ruined Reeboks. All in all, it had been a pretty good wreck.

The rain got steadily worse as the day wore on and the wrecks increased. There was a bad wreck in the south end of the county that the Highway Patrol called us on and I sent Mike out to help handle that. Fifteen minutes later, Gladys came in to say there was a disturbance out at Holiday Hell in Bishop.

Dalton was back at work, but his gunshot shoulder had him doing desk duty, and since Mike was out at the south end of the county, I took the call and headed north to Bishop. The manager of the trailer court had called it in. Shouts and general mayhem coming from trailer number five, which wasn't all that far from Edna Earle Moon's trailer, and I couldn't help glancing over there as I parked the car and got out, taking the nightstick from my belt and holding it in my hand. I knocked smartly on the door of trailer number five, then knocked again, louder.

Finally, the door opened and a beefy, long-haired man dressed in dirty jeans and a tank top with a snake tattoo on his upper arm stood staring down at me.

"What the fuck you want?" he asked.

"Manager called in a disturbance," I said, showing him my badge, even though I was dressed in uniform and he shoulda figured that out, but the guy didn't look none too bright.

"So?" he asked belligerently.

"So mind if I ask what's going on here?"

"Yeah, I mind!" he said, starting to slam the door.

I stuck the nightstick in the doorway, blocking his slam, moved quickly up the aluminum steps of the trailer and threw my shoulder into the door. It banged open, shoving the snake-tattooed fella back into the room.

A young woman lay on the floor, her mouth bleeding. I said, "Ma'am? You okay?"

She sat up and rubbed at her face. "Jesus, does it look like I'm okay?"

"Shut up, Bambi!" Snake Tattoo said.

"Go fuck yourself, George!" she screamed. "You didn't have no right to hit me!" Whereupon she jumped up and began pounding him in the face with her fists.

I got between them and sat them both down. "Now lookee here," I said. "Ma'am, you wanna press charges against this man?"

George sat on the couch, his face in his hands. When he looked up at her, tears were streaming down his face. "Baby, I'm sorry!" he wailed.

Bambi jumped up and ran around me, throwing her arms around his neck. "Oh, honey! You know that prick don't mean nothing to me! I love *you*, Georgie, only you!"

George gulped in air. "Don't sleep with him no more, okay, baby?"

Bambi ruffled his hair. "I promise, baby, I promise I won't never sleep with him again."

I moved toward the door of the trailer. "Well, if you two are calmed down enough, and, ma'am, if you're sure you don't want to press charges—"

"Just get the fuck out, pig!" she said. "Nobody called you for nothing!"

Well, somebody did, but I didn't feel like staying around and arguing the point. I took the two steps down to the ground and headed in the rain for my squad car. It wasn't until I got in that I saw Lonnette Moon sitting in the passenger side.

"Well, hey, Lonnette," I said.

She smiled briefly, a small twist at the sides of her mouth. "Hey, Sheriff," she said.

"What are you doing in my car, honey?" I asked.

"I thought you come for me," she said, staring straight ahead at the rain through the windshield of the car.

"Now why would I do that?" I asked.

"Because I kilt my daddy," she said.

◀ 18 ▶

I started the engine of the squad car and backed away from trailer number five, then turned and headed out of the trailer park.

"Don't tell me any more, Lonnette," I said. "I don't want you to say a word." But since she didn't seem to be about to say anything, I figured that was one of those moot points you read about in books.

We drove in silence to the station where I deposited Lonnette with Gladys with instructions for neither of 'em to talk, and got on the phone. First I called Bill Williams in Tejas County suggesting he get his shiny ass over here as quick as can be, then I called the Bishop Elementary and asked to speak to Edna Earle Moon, telling them it was an emergency.

When Edna Earle got on the line, I said, "Miz Moon, this is Sheriff Kovak. Lonnette is down here at the sheriff's department and I think you best get on down here too, ma'am."

Edna Earle didn't say anything. Just hung up. I sat and stared off into space for fifteen minutes or so, until all hell broke loose.

First the door opened and Edna Earle Moon walked in. She sat down in one of my visitor's chairs, crossed her legs at the ankles, and folded her hands in her lap. "Sheriff, I would like to confess to killing my former husband, Wade Norvell Moon the Second."

"Norvell?" I said.

Then the door opened again and Gayla Moon walked in, didn't even glance at Edna Earle, walked straight to my desk, put her hands on it, and leaned forward. "Milt, I killed Wade," she said.

Then the door opened and Bill walked in. I said, "Bill, my man, why don't you go to the office next door, my former office, and bring you in a chair. Thanks kindly." To Gayla, I said, "Honey, why don't you sit down here next to Edna Earle. You two know each other?"

Neither said a word. "That why your beat-up old Chevy pickup was in Gayla's daddy's driveway when Bill and me were there last week?" I asked.

Neither said a word.

Bill drug the chair in. I said, "Bill, would you mind reading these ladies their rights?"

"Huh?" he said.

"Please," I said.

Bill pulled the little Miranda card out of his shirt pocket and read it to them, stumbling a bit, backing up once, but getting it all out in one piece.

"Now," I said to the two women, "do you understand these rights as Deputy Williams has read them to you?"

Both women nodded.

"Would you say that out loud, please?" I asked.

Both women said, "Yes."

I looked at Bill and he nodded, confirming that he had heard them acknowledge their rights.

"Okay, Gayla," I said, "you wanna call your daddy?"

She shook her head. "No, Milt. Daddy can't do me much good now."

"Sheriff," Edna Earle said.

"Yes, Miz Moon?"

"I want to repeat to you that I kilt my former husband, Wade Norvell Moon the Second."

"No, she didn't," Gayla said. "I killed Wade."

I looked over at Bill, whose eyes were big as saucers. "Now, Deputy Williams, just to keep the record straight, I would like to inform you that Lonnette Moon, the daughter of Miz Edna Earle Moon, has confessed to killing Wade Moon also."

"Whoa, shit," he said.

"Yes, sir," I said, "my sentiments exactly." I turned back to the two women. "Would one of you like to tell me what's going on?"

"I kilt Wade because he wouldn't give me money," Edna Earle said, still sitting as primly as ever.

"Edna Earle, don't," Gayla said, touching one of the hands in Edna Earle's lap. Edna Earle moved her hand and clasped Gayla's hand in hers.

"Girl," she said, squeezing Gayla's hand. "You go on home to your daddy. I'll take care of this here."

Gayla shook her head and I saw tears in her eyes. "No, Edna Earle. I killed Wade and I'll take the blame for it."

Edna Earle let go of Gayla's hand and looked at me. "I kilt Wade Moon," she said, going back to her prim pose.

"Why?" I asked.

"Because he wouldn't pay me no child support," she said.

"Why did you kill him, Gayla?" I asked.

"Because . . . because . . . oh, God!" Gayla Moon burst into tears, her hands to her face, sobbing. Edna Earle turned to her, drawing her head to her shoulder.

"Hush, child," she said, rubbing Gayla's back. "He's gone, that's all that matters."

Bill and I stood by, mute audience to the drama that was Wade Moon's women. Finally, Gayla took a handkerchief out of her purse and dried her face. Looking at Edna Earle, she said, "We've got to tell the truth." Looking at me, she said, "If we tell you the truth, will you both keep it secret? Not tell anyone?"

I shook my head. "Gayla, when this thing goes to court—"

"It won't go to court. We've both already confessed, what more do you need? Why should it go to court?"

Bill stood up and moved to stand behind my chair. He touched my shoulder. "Milt, I think we need to hear them out."

Maybe somewhere in me I knew what was coming. Maybe that's why I didn't want them to tell the truth. But Bill was right. And so was Gayla. It was time the truth came out.

I nodded my head.

Gayla looked at Edna Earle, who looked down at her hands and said nothing.

Taking a deep breath, Gayla said, "I met Wade Moon when I was eight years old. He used to take my girlfriend and me home from school. At first, it was just once a week, then it became more often. Then he started dropping Dorey off and he and I would drive around together and talk." She took a deep breath. "He started touching me, telling me it was our game and nobody could know about it because it would make them mad and they'd hurt both of us. On my ninth birthday . . ." She took a deep breath and a sob choked her throat. "On my ninth birthday he . . . he took me to the woods . . . he . . ."

Edna Earle put her arm around Gayla's shoulders. Gayla looked into her eyes, seeming to find some strength there, and said, "On my ninth birthday Wade Moon raped me. This behavior continued until I was sixteen and we ran away together." She looked at me. "You asked a question while you were at my parents' house last week. You asked me why Wade retired so early. It was because he'd been doing it again. Four girls in our neighborhood, from the ages of six to twelve. One of the girls told and it was beginning to come out. So we came back here."

Edna Earle patted Gayla's hand and smiled at her. Looking at me, she said, "Wade and me was cousins, did you know that, Milt?"

I shook my head. "No, ma'am, I didn't know that."

"I was twenty-five years old and a spinster, according to the way things were where we come from, Storeytown, Arkansas. Wade was eighteen. He been caught messing with young girls and the family thought he best be married off quick 'fore the law got on to him. We was third cousins so they married me off to him and the family sent us to Longbranch to live with Uncle Marsh who had a piece of land up here. Wade worked the land for a while and I got pregnant with Lonnette. Then Uncle Marsh died and his land went to the county 'cause he hadn't paid taxes in about ten years so Wade got the job with the county sheriff."

She looked at me and I nodded. She continued. "Lonnette was a sweet baby. No trouble atall from that child. Always cooing and playing with her toes and such. Never one to make a fuss about much. After the baby—" Edna Earle looked down and I could see pink tinging her skin. Defiantly, she looked straight at me and said, "After the baby, Wade didn't fulfill his husband duties no more. I didn't say nothing about it because I wasn't raised that way. I know women on Oprah and stuff talk about that all the time, but I wasn't raised that way."

"Yes, ma'am, I understand," I said.

"I want you to know, Milt, that nobody in the family told me the kinda trouble Wade was in when they married me off to him. They just said trouble and I thought it was probably moonshine 'cause my daddy and both my brothers got sent to the federal pen for that. I didn't know until . . . later, when I called back to Storeytown and ast." She shook her head. "I can only guess that when Wade wasn't fulfilling his husband duties with me, he was probably messing with young girls around here." She shook her head. "I didn't know." Taking a deep breath, she said, "The reason Wade run off with Gayla thirteen years ago is 'cause . . . Lonnette come on with child. When I saw it, I said, 'Girl, who's been messing with you?' But, Lonnette, she's simple, and she didn't understand. When I made it real clear to her what I meant . . . she said . . . 'Oh, Mama, only Daddy. I'd only do that with Daddy.' "

Bill walked away from behind my desk and sat heavily down in the chair he'd vacated earlier. I looked at the blotter on my desk, unable to look at either of the women.

"When Wade come home that night, I told him. Told him what Lonnette said. I yelled at him. I never done that before. He just got up and went into the bedroom and packed a suitcase and walked out the door."

"He didn't tell me about Lonnette," Gayla said. "He never said a word about either of them. Just picked me up from school and said, 'We're leaving.' Just like that."

We all sat quietly for a moment, thinking about the past and the horrors in it. Finally, Edna Earle said, "I moved out of the house and moved to the trailer in Bishop. I took Lonnette out of school then. Kept her in the trailer. I wore padding under my clothes to make me look like I was with child. I delivered Tula myself." She shook her head. "Poor Lonnette. She didn't know what was happening. She was only 'bout twelve years old herself. She kept screaming, 'Mama, I'm dying. I'm dying!" Edna Earle shook her head. "I got that baby out of her and gave her some sleeping pills. The next day I told her I had a baby. She didn't know no better."

"I didn't know when we left town, but I was pregnant, too," Gayla said. Edna Earle's hand covered Gayla's, squeezing. The two women looked at each other, then Gayla turned back to me. "I was scared to death, Milt, when I found out." She sighed. "A girl in my class had gotten pregnant the year before and she'd taken care of it herself. She was afraid to go to an abortion clinic, and couldn't get a ride to the nearest one, anyway. And then there was parental consent . . . Anyway, she'd told me and another girl exactly what she'd done. So I did that. Wade came home and I was bleeding so bad . . ." A sob caught in her throat. "He was so angry. Called me a murderer. He threw me in the bedroom of that little apartment we were staying in and he pulled the phone out of the wall and said I could just stay there until I knew what a horrible person I was. He locked me in there for almost twenty-four hours. When he came to check on me, I could barely move my head. I'd stuffed all the towels we had between my legs, and they were soaked with blood. He finally took me to the hospital. On the way there, he told me not to tell anyone what I'd done or they'd know how evil I was." She sighed and looked down at her hands. "He said it was God's punishment that I was so messed up I couldn't have any more babies. But one of the nurses told me that if I'd gotten there sooner, I probably would have been okay."

Gayla stood up. "Milt, the minute we moved back here, he saw Tula. He started talking about how beautiful she was. How special. His special little girl." She choked back a sob. "Well, Milt, I was his 'special little girl' once. I knew what that meant so I killed him."

Edna Earle stood up. "He started coming by and seeing Tula. He would rub her back in front of me, talk about what a sweet baby she was. I knew what he was gonna do, so I kilt him."

The door opened and Lonnette walked in, followed by a frantic Gladys. "Milt, I couldn't stop her—" Gladys started.

"It's okay," I said. "Shut the door."

Gladys shut the door, leaving Lonnette in the room with us. "Mama," Lonnette said, "when we going home?"

"In a minute, baby," Edna Earle said, stroking Lonnette's arm.

"Mama, I told the sheriff I kilt Daddy," Lonnette said.

"Why, Lonnette?" I asked.

She looked at me. Her dull blue eyes misted over. " 'Cause he was gonna hurt Tula like he hurt me. Mama, I didn't want him to hurt Tula."

"I know, baby, I know," Edna Earle said, stroking Lonnette's arm. To me, she said, "I kilt Wade Moon, Milt, and ain't nobody ever gonna say different."

"I killed him, Milt," Gayla said.

"Did you two do this together?" Bill asked.

"No!" they both said.

"I thought it up and I did it all by myself," Edna Earle said.

"I got up that morning when he did and followed him out to the lake," Gayla said, "and told him I'd like to go fishing with him and then I hit him with the oar—"

"And swam back to shore?" I asked.

"Yes," Gayla said, sitting down.

"No," Edna Earle said. "I met him there. Said I needed to talk about the girls. He took me out in the boat—"

"Lonnette," I said, "what happened when you killed your daddy? Where were you?"

Edna Earle stood in front of her daughter. "Now, Sheriff—"

"Edna Earle," I said gently. "Let the girl speak."

Lonnette sat down in the chair vacated by her mother. "He been messing with Tula that night," she said. "Touching at her. Stuff like that. Made me think. Made me remember stuff I didn't wanna think about."

"I understand," I said.

"So next morning, early, I got up . . . Mama," she said, turning and looking up at Edna Earle, "I know I ain't supposed to leave the trailer, but I was getting itchy—"

"It's okay, baby," Edna Earle said, stroking Lonnette's hair.

"I just went walking. I just walked and walked. Then my daddy was there in his shiny red car and he ast me what I was doing and I told him thinking. He said come think in his car so I did. He ast me did I wanna go fishing with him and I said okay. Then we get out on the water and he start touching my leg under my nightgown and I tole him no, but he wouldn't stop, so I hit him and made him stop."

Edna Earle stroked her hair. "Hush, baby," she said. "Hush, now."

Bill stood up. "Milt, I need some fresh air. Join me?"

I stood and followed Bill out of the room, down the back hall to the side door, and out into the parking lot.

"I'm dropping the case, Milt," he said. "Ain't no way I'm bringing charges against any one of them three."

I studied the asphalt beneath my feet. "They didn't have to kill him," I said. "They coulda turned him in."

"Yeah, right," Bill said, studying the clouds in the sky. "And pray somebody could keep him from touching Tula."

We stood and stared off into space for a while, neither one willing to look at the other, then walked back inside.

Bill and I went into my office where the three women sat.

"I got one question to ask," I said.

The two older women nodded and Lonnette looked at me quizzically.

"Which one of you put a bomb in my car and then shot my deputy?"

Gayla looked at Edna Earle. Edna Earle looked at Lonnette. All three shook their heads. "Milt," Gayla said, "we had nothing to do with that. I promise you."

Bill said, "Ladies, I don't seem to have enough evidence to charge anyone with a crime here, so if you three wouldn't mind, we're just going to chalk this one up to person or persons unknown."

Gayla and Edna Earle stood up. Lonnette followed her mama's lead. "We can go?" Gayla asked.

I motioned to the door. "One thing, though," I said. All three looked back. "My wife is a psychiatrist, runs the psychiatric unit at the hospital. I think the three of you should talk to her. I think that real strong."

Gayla nodded. "I'll see to it, Milt," she said, then all three left.

Bill and I sat in my office for a spell, neither talking, neither looking at each other. Guilty by association.

Finally, Bill said, "Milt, I got a daughter my ownself."

I nodded. "I know that, Bill."

"I'da killed him with my bare hands. Slow and easy. Hurt him so bad his grandpa'd bleed—"

"Bill," I said.

He stood up, walked to the door, opened it and, without turning back to look at me, said, "Case closed."

I didn't do much the rest of the afternoon. Just stared out the window at the intermittent rain. And thought about Wade Moon. My friend. Eight or sixteen, Gayla had still been a baby. I'd known about him messing with her when she was sixteen, and I hadn't done a damn thing about it. He'd been in his midthirties then. Messing with a sixteen-year-old girl. That shoulda told me something. Told me something was wrong. But she'd been so damned beautiful I'd thought about it myself. To my shame.

Around 4:30 I grabbed my car coat, put it on, and, bidding Gladys good night, headed out the side door to my Jeep. The shot came out of nowhere. Hit me in the middle of the chest and knocked me clear across the asphalt into the cinder block side of the building.

◀ 19 ▶

I scrambled to my feet, holding on to the wall for support. My chest hurt so bad I thought I'd die. Looking up, I saw the pickup across the street, the rifle aimed at me again. Mike Neils' squad car came from around the corner and crashed into the side of the pickup. I hobbled over toward the mess as Mike got out of his car, service revolver leveled at the man behind the wheel, who was leaning over, his head lolling against the steering wheel.

I got there as Mike gingerly opened the driver's door. Pulling the head up by the hair, he exposed the face of my assailant. The man who'd put a bomb in my car, shot Dalton in the shoulder, and tried to gut-shoot me. All because of what was little more than a practical joke. Clifford Reynolds.

Jean stood on her crutches next to the bed in the emergency room while the young intern taped my ribs. I had three of the suckers broken. And a bruise bigger than Texas in the center of my chest, radiating out to both underdeveloped pecs. It was not a pretty sight. Of course, without the vest, it would have been a little bit worse. Like no chest at all. Just a big hole with my innards counted among the missing.

"He was obviously unstable, Milt," Jean said, trying to help me deal with the guilt I felt over the whole damn thing. If I'd just left it alone. Just given the girls their own party and let the tight-assed bastard live with his prejudices, then my '55 would be purring like a kitten and Dalton Pettigrew would have two good arms and be driving around in a squad car. Business as usual. And Clifford Reynolds wouldn't be in the hospital with a concussion and a jail sentence looming over his head. Maxine Reynolds wouldn't be losing a husband and Mindy Reynolds wouldn't be losing her daddy.

But I hadn't done that. Nope, not Milton "Gotta stick your nose in it" Kovak.

Jean touched my shoulder. "If it hadn't been this and you, Milt, it would have been something else. At some point. A rational person doesn't react the way Clifford Reynolds reacted."

"Yeah," I said, "well, a rational person doesn't hound somebody the way I did him, neither."

She smiled at me. "I see you'd like to wallow in this awhile," she said.

I didn't say anything. My thoughts were not ones I wanted to share at this point.

We drove home together in Jean's car. We were silent part of the way, then I said, "I'm handing in my shield."

Jean turned to look at me. That's one thing about a psychiatrist. She didn't even look surprised. "And why is that?" she asked evenly.

"I ain't got no right being sheriff. I threw Elberry out of his job for doing the same thing I just did. Abusing his authority. I took advantage of my situation and ended up almost killing a big, dumb lug like Dalton. I'm gonna cost the state a bunch of money feeding and housing Clifford Reynolds for the next few years, not to mention the cost of his trial. And all because I got my feelings hurt. And abused my authority."

"So you're quitting?"

I sighed. "Yes, ma'am," I said, looking out the window at the dark clouds building up to the north. Almost as dark as the clouds building up around my soul.

"I wish you'd think about it for a while, Milt. If you think about it rationally, I think you'll see that what you did does not equate with what Elberry did. He willingly put people's lives in jeopardy covering a wrong. You, unwittingly, put people's lives in jeopardy trying to right a wrong. There is a difference."

"Not that I can see," I said, not looking at her.

In an attempt to change the subject, I told her what had happened that day with the Wade Moon case. Ending with, "So I asked them to come see you. I'll follow up on that before I do anything about my job. I'll make sure they come see you."

"Which one do you think did it?" Jean asked.

I sighed. "Lonnette. I know she did it. She's the only one without the guile to lie. Edna Earle's obviously covering for her. And I think that's what Gayla's doing too."

"Why would Gayla cover for her?" Jean asked.

"You're the shrink, not me, but . . ."

Jean smiled. "Go for it, big guy," she said.

"Okay. Gayla hated Wade. She'd been trapped by him since she was eight years old. He had a hold over her she couldn't break." I thought for a moment. "She couldn't go to her daddy for help. Knowing him the way I do, which admittedly ain't much, I'd say he'd be the kinda guy who'd kill Wade, then blame Gayla for it the rest of her life."

Jean nodded.

"She wanted Wade dead, but she never had the nerve to do it. He'd abused her since she was a child. Ruined her only chance to have children. When he was dead, maybe she thought her wishing had done it. Maybe she got together with Edna Earle and found out what happened. I truly believe she didn't want Tula to go through what she had gone through. And she didn't want Lonnette to suffer any more than she already had."

Jean nodded. "And there's the possibility that admitting to Wade's murder was a way of getting a handle on the guilt she felt for the abuse and the abortion."

"You think?" I asked.

"The human mind is an incredibly tricky thing, Milt," she said. "What's going to happen to Lonnette?" she asked as she pulled into our long driveway.

"That's up to you, honey," I said. "If you think she'll be a danger to anyone else, I'll see to it that Edna Earle has her put away. A nice private place. Someplace pretty."

"Edna Earle hasn't got the money for that," Jean said, pulling to a stop.

I thought about the money burning a hole in the top shelf of my closet. "There are resources," I said. "We don't have to worry about that."

"When are you going to hand in your badge?" she asked.

"I don't know," I said, staring out the window at my house.

"Why don't you do this," Jean said, taking my hand in hers and pressing it against the swell of her belly. "Why don't you wait until April. If you don't win the election, then the decision will be moot. If you do win—well, then worry about it."

I looked at her. Then looked down at the swell of her belly. "I'm running unopposed," I said.

She lifted my hand to her lips and kissed it. "You never know what's going to happen," Jean said, smiling at me. "Why don't we just wait and see?"

I nodded, kissed her lightly on the mouth, and we both got out of the car, heading for the front door. When we opened it, I almost headed for the phone to call for backup. The whole house had been ransacked. The living room furniture was in a pile on the floor, all the pictures taken down, the curtains, the knick-knacks. In the kitchen, boxes sat everywhere, full of utensils and dishes and whatnot. Suspecting it had little to do with burglars, Jean and I walked into the nursery.

All the furniture was gone. The walls were back to basic white, the teddy bear wallpaper gone. Sitting in the middle of the floor was the cradle. In it was a piece of paper.

I picked it up and handed it to Jean, then read over her shoulder:

> This cradle was made for me before I was born by Milton and my daddy. All three of my children were nurtured and nested in this cradle. I would like very much to pass it on to the two of you. Jean, I'm sorry. If someone had done to me what I did to you, my reaction would have been as strong if not stronger than yours. I want you to know, though, I was only trying to help. Sometimes I get carried away.
>
> Jewel

Jean walked out of the nursery and to the phone in the foyer, picked it up and dialed. From my hiding place in the dining room, I heard her say, "Hi, Jewel. Thanks." There was a pause and then she laughed, pulled up a chair and sat down for a chat.

I smiled and went into the kitchen to wonder where my bride might want to keep the silverware.